Trouble
In
Tulum

Trouble in Tulum

The Divine Drama Exposed

A Novel

Judith Whitman-Small

and

Diana Cooper

≡⌂≡
Ashland Hills Press
Ashland, Oregon

TROUBLE IN TULUM *is a work of fiction. Any resemblance its characters, events and descriptions may bear to actual persons, events, organizations or other entities is entirely coincidental and unintended.*

Cover adapted from an original oil painting, "The Ecstasy," by Judith Whitman-Small

Cover design by Katy Tisch

Adaptation of Mayan glyphs by Gwen Cooper

Typeset in Bookman Old Style

Library of Congress Control Number: 2004115240

ISBN 0-9642272-2-3

First Edition.

Published by Ashland Hills Press, P.O. Box 992, Ashland, OR 97520, USA, Phone 541-951-1129

Printed in the United States of America by CDS Printing, Medford, Oregon

Dedicated to the Divine Mystery
From which everything arises.

Preface

The Enneagram is an insightful and potentially transformative system of delineating and describing nine basic expressions of human nature. It is a system which is widely applied in the field of psychology today.

Trouble in Tulum is not intended as a serious treatment of this highly respected form of personality interpretation. We have used the Enneagram as a loose frame of reference for creating the characters in our book, much as actors are cast for a play. With a light-hearted touch, we gave birth to the characters. Once imbued with life, they seriously assumed their roles, playing them with total conviction in the Divine Drama until, well, you'll see.

Although the characters are inspired by the Enneagram, our book is actually about awakening from the trance of identification with a limited persona, into the realization of our true nature.

None of the individuals in this book are intentionally meant to represent any person or persons, although the authors found elements of their own personalities portrayed in every one of the characters. We fell in love with all of them and we hope you will too.

TROUBLE IN TULUM

The Divine Drama Exposed

The Cast of Characters

Maya Llusion - a spiritual workshop leader. In the Divine Drama she embodies the belief of separation from Source and is a master at perpetuating the illusion of an individual self.

Quantomundi - a Mayan shaman.

The Enneagram - Nine variations of the Divine expression, which if not seen as a problem, can be highly entertaining and celebrated.

The Nine Enneagram Character Fixations

Number One: C King - Ones are motivated by the need to live an idealized life. They can be self-righteous and judgmental but are also ethical, wise and generous.

Number Two: Betty Butterup - Twos want to be loved and appreciated. They sometimes flatter others and give expecting something in return. They can be caring, generous and insightful.

Number Three: Govinda Go Go - Threes derive a large part of their identity from accomplishment. They are ambitious, confident, optimistic, and excel in motivating others

Number Four: Mona Preen - Fours are afraid of being anonymous and ordinary. They often focus on their image and have a sense of entitlement. They can be intuitive, creative and compassionate.

Number Five: Ivanta B. Alone - Fives like to feel self-sufficient. They have a need to understand everything. They can be stubborn but are also perceptive, sensitive and wise.

Number Six: Pere Anoiananda - Sixes are motivated by the need to feel safe. They often have a difficult time making decisions and look outside themselves for approval. They can be loyal, supportive and caring.

Number Seven: Wu Wu Way - Sevens are motivated by the need to feel happy and avoid anything uncomfortable. They can be rather narcissistic but are also spontaneous, charming and fun-loving.

Number Eight: Baba Bossysatva - Eights need to be self-reliant and strong. They like to be in charge and can be overbearing. They are loyal, protective and earthy.

Number Nine: Sita Sofa - Nines are motivated by the need to keep the peace. They can procrastinate and are self-narcotizing. They are empathic, generous and open-minded.

Supporting Cast

Inspector Hidalgo Neti Neti

Sergeant Salvadore Shadow

Chief Detective Ramon Stompedo

Sergeant Juan Abee

Eduardo Vargas, staff at the Ah So Retreat Center

Arturo Salinas, staff at the Ah So Retreat Center

Prologue

THE INTENSE MIDDAY SUN reflected off the hood of an old Tulum taxi as it rolled to a stop in front of the Ah So Retreat Center. Shifting shadows from lush tropical vegetation cast intricate patterns across the landscape as an imposing looking woman emerged from the cab. A sea breeze played with the layers of veils that enveloped her, sending them swirling in a profusion of purple and magenta. The air was charged with her presence as she threw off any trace of travel fatigue and issued a directive to the driver concerning her luggage.

Then, intent, and with a regal air, she strode off to the nearby cliff overlooking the sea. Surveying the landscape, she recognized the famous Tulum ruins nearby and moved resolutely toward them.

When she reached the ancient site, she proceeded

with great purpose to the highest point of land. Cliffs of intriguing rock formations dropped dramatically to the sea below. She gazed out at the horizon, where the sky merged with the vastness of the ocean and, at first, found herself spellbound by the beauty of the place. An all-pervasive sense of timelessness engulfed her. But then, quite suddenly, that sensation morphed into something else, something distinctly unpleasant. She began to feel disoriented, threatened even, as though she'd somehow lost her boundaries. Her chest felt tight and she could scarcely catch her breath. She feared she might faint right there on the spot.

Pull yourself together, Maya, she told herself firmly. *Remember why you're here in Tulum among these ancient ruins. It's an established fact that this is a place of immense power.*

Slowly, she regained her equilibrium. Remembering she'd come to Tulum on a mission restored her sense of purpose and control. Maya Llusion opened her arms wide and declared majestically, "*This* is the place."

ACT I

Let the Play Begin

INSPECTOR HIDALGO NETI NETI walked the wide beach, leaving a trail of footprints in the warm sand. He was a small man with large ambition, eager to prove himself.

He paused, looking up at the cliff where the Ah So Retreat Center's expansive windows gleamed in the morning sun. The center, adjacent to the Tulum ruins, was uniquely situated on a rocky point overlooking the Caribbean Sea.

I wonder what they actually do up there? Neti Neti had been told it was one of those New Age centers where workshops of some sort took place. *What a lot of nonsense. Maybe Sergeant Shadow and I should visit the bar tonight, see if the place is on the up and up.*

Neti Neti's latest assignment for the past few months was to patrol the Tulum area. He was bored to distraction. He was to watch for cocaine trafficking, the only blemish that marred this paradise located midway along the eastern coast of the Yucatan Peninsula. With the exception of one minor drug drop-off by boat, the inspector had had little opportunity to display his investigative expertise and razor-sharp mind. Thus far, all his energies had been wasted picking up bits of trash along the two-mile stretch of shoreline, all the while scanning the sea for suspicious looking craft. Persistent thoughts of a major drug bust and its attending glory fanned his frustration.

■ □ ■

At that very moment, at the Ah So Retreat Center, spiritual-seekers were tumbling out of hot, dusty shuttles and moving toward the shaded lobby. The air was filled with voices charged with anticipation and a certain giddiness which masked the participants' underlying anxiety. The weekend intensive had been advertised as a once-in-a-lifetime opportunity to expand one's spiritual power, but there'd been precious little detail about the methods to be used.

Maya Llusion, the workshop leader, was a legendary figure rumored in New Age circles to be the ultimate teacher. Her curriculum, shrouded in secrecy, kept this perception alive.

Stories abounded regarding this mysterious woman. It was said that Maya Llusion's teachings were at times ruthless and unconventional, and this approach appealed to many frustrated seekers who had exhausted most other paths to enlightenment. Many of her students left her workshops definitely "rearranged" and believing themselves to be a few rungs higher on the ladder to spiritual success.

IN THE LOBBY, NINE SPIRITUAL SEEKERS waited in line to check in.

Miss Betty Butterup, a perky, voluptuous blonde, turned as she recognized a familiar laugh coming from across the lobby. She made a beeline for the source of this laughter, leaving a trail of overturned luggage and startled workshop participants, whom she had shoved aside in her fervor.

"Oh, Wu Wu Way," she gushed, rapidly moving in for a full body hug. Seeing Wu Wu's doubtful expression, she nevertheless pressed on, "Surely you remember me from the 'Awakening Your Kundalini Intensive' in Sheboygan?"

"Ah, yes," he replied, swiveling his body to avoid her grasp. "But I didn't see you at the 'Past Life Recovery Program' in Death Valley last January." With a slightly condescending air, he added, "Are you signed up for the 'Full Moon Chakra Rotation Ritual' in July?"

Somewhat deflated, Betty reminded herself, but did not share with Wu Wu, that she'd been dramatically impacted by her last workshop, "Discovering the Barbie Within." Now she had every hope the breast enhancement and waist cincher would pay off for her big-time. She quickly pulled from her pocket an inexpensive but impressive looking amulet and pressed it into Wu Wu's hand. "I want you to have this," she said seductively, "and to remember me as you wear it."

"Oh," cooed Wu Wu, "this will go with the one I picked up in Machu Picchu two weeks ago." He rewarded her with a tentative smile.

A slender man slipped behind the reception counter, ready for business. He self-consciously ran his hand over his slicked back hair and delicately fingered a small, black goatee. Then, after carefully arranging the papers before him, Eduardo Vargas looked up and greeted the first guest in line.

"Name please?" he said. His gaze met the intense, hawkish glare of Mrs. C. King, who peered down at him through half-glasses perched precariously on the tip of her considerable nose. She was a tall matron with seemingly great force of character.

"I hope this place lives up to the description in the brochure," were her first skeptical words. "I'll need to check out my room to make certain it's adequate."

Ignoring this, Eduardo pushed a guest registration form across the counter and handed her a pen. "Please fill this out and sign here."

C. King's face flushed with barely concealed displeasure as she complied and was then handed a large key marked 'Number 14.' Lips pursed, she moved through the lobby toward the patio.

Eduardo had endured this exchange over the drone of conversation among the others in line, in particular a monologue interspersed with large guffaws of pleasure. A woman of significant girth, whose neatly stacked chins moved in unison as she talked, was next in line. So absorbed in her saga did she appear, with all its meanderings and irrelevancies, that she failed to notice that those around her had completely lost interest, or that it was her turn to check in.

Eduardo cleared his throat noisily. "Madame?"

The monologue ceased and after some fumbling in a large woven bag, the woman stepped forward and handed Eduardo her passport. "What are your mattresses like? I like a *very* soft one and I'll need a television in my room with viewing from the bed. I hope I can catch my favorite programs. Oh, by the way," she said with a self-deprecating laugh, "I'm Sita Sofa. I almost didn't get my application in on time, but here I am! I hope you're serving fresh seafood for dinner tonight?"

Eduardo suggested she consult the menu in the dining room and handed her a pen. "Please fill this out and sign here."

Sita completed the registration form and ambled away, heading for the hammock out on the patio. She moved somewhat furtively toward it.

"I really need a great deal of privacy," the next guest insisted in a hushed, cultured voice. She was a slim attractive woman in dark sunglasses with a self-contained, no-nonsense manner. Given directions to the most remote dwelling on the property, Ivanta B. Alone signed the registration form and, hoisting her only piece of luggage, a sleek duffel bag, made her way out into the bright morning sun.

Next, a diminutive character with darting eyes stepped cautiously up to the counter. Pere Anoiananda was clearly not at ease. In fact, Eduardo could not recall ever having seen a more anxious looking man. *I wonder what's got him so undone?*

As Eduardo handed him the key to his accommodations, Pere said in an almost inaudible voice, "Does anyone else have a key to my room? I don't want anyone coming in—just leave the clean linens outside." He glanced anxiously from side to side to see if anyone was listening, then snatched his suitcase and headed out the door.

Eduardo acknowledged the next guest, a Miss Mona Preen, according to her passport. Her elegant appearance was flawless and the result was effective. Her clothes were unique, and her flowing hair, a rich chestnut brown, had no doubt been expensively tweaked. Surrounded by many pieces of designer luggage, Mona presented herself.

"I require a room with a dramatic view, large closets and a modern bath with full-length mirrors."

Eduardo sighed. "Madame, this is rural Mexico. We

offer small individual guest houses—*palapas*—with thatched roofs and spasmodic electricity. You will occasionally share your room with geckos and the odd spider." It was hardly what this guest was demanding, he knew. Eduardo went on to answer Miss Preen's questions. Then, with key in hand and chin high, she followed a procession of porters out the door.

Eduardo looked up with admirable resignation to greet the next weekend guest. Miss Betty Butterup leaned toward Eduardo, breathlessly introduced herself and handed over her passport. After signing the registry, she sensuously slipped the key from his moist palm and bestowed a smile. His dark eyes glistened as he directed her to her *palapa*.

Wu Wu Way, a tall, slender man whose handsome face was somewhat hampered by a weak chin, appeared most anxious to get to his room. He gave Eduardo no trouble; he simply handed over his passport, signed the requisite forms, grabbed his key and hurried off.

The next man, Baba Bossysatva according to his passport, was apparently unaccustomed to waiting in line. His anger must have been building during his wait, and he now unleashed its full fury on Eduardo. "Where in the *world* did they find someone like you?" he said contemptuously. He hurriedly completed the forms, snatched his key and strode off.

The last of the nine guests stepped forward—Govinda Go Go, an energetic, middle-aged man with a youthful, unlived-in face. "This all seems pretty inefficient," he informed Eduardo as he handed over his passport. He hurriedly completed the required forms. Then his cell phone rang and he began speaking into it, only half-listening as Eduardo gave him his key and attempted to offer directions to his *palapa*. Eduardo overheard something about a merger as the man moved off.

As BABA BOSSYSATVA made his way to his *palapa*, his impatience with the long wait in line faded, for the scene surrounding him was stunning. The sound of the blue-green sea was constant in the background. White sand paths lined with red and pink hibiscus, bougainvillea and tall palm trees led in all directions to the guest houses. Two large dome-shaped buildings with thatched roofs dominated the property. According to the map Eduardo had given him, these were an open-air dining room and bar, and the meeting hall. The beauty of the place caught Bossy off guard. For one brief moment he had a sense of there being no boundary between himself and the world around him, and then, just as suddenly, there was a separate world again. He stood rooted to the spot, amazed.

■ □ ■

Wu Wu Way was eager to get to his room to balance his energy and fluff his aura after the long trip, which he felt had exposed him to some seriously negative energies. He opened the door to his *palapa* to find a pleasant room with large windows facing the ocean. He unzipped one of his bags and began placing a collection of crystals on the low table under the front window. *The intense tropical sun should charge these nicely.* Next, he unpacked his recently purchased *chi* machine, Tarot deck, fresh vegetable juicer and a container of dietary fiber.

He had a strong feeling that being in Tulum was part of a grand cosmic plan. He would need to make phone calls *immediately*, to cancel the few options he had left open in case the Tulum retreat turned out not to be stimulating enough. *I can always pick those up later,* he thought excitedly.

In a glowing mood, he finished unpacking and went out into the brilliant sunlight to find a phone.

■ □ ■

Muttering, and still trying to figure out what had possessed him to come to Tulum, Pere Anoiananda made his way to his *palapa*, scanning the surrounding area for possible lurking danger. Fear of injury via some unpleasant and possibly violent means segued into visions of large tropical insects invading his bed at night. How would he ever manage to relax in this unfamiliar tropical terrain? Certainly those odd, heavily foliated bushes would be perfect lairs for venomous snakes. The entire area was probably teeming with reptiles and aggressive monkeys and Lord knows what else. He'd have to constantly be on the alert for scorpions that might creep into his empty shoes at night. *Yes, it was insanity to have come.*

Relax, he heard a voice say.

Who was that? he wondered, certain there was no one nearby.

His mental soliloquy continued: *Should I ask for a room nearer the meeting hall? Did I pack the flashlight? Oh, God! Maybe I left it on the hall table at home.*

Home seemed so far away now, and so safe. With a bitter feeling of having somehow been tricked into coming to the workshop, he found his hand on the door to his room. He opened it, entered, shut it firmly behind him and leaned against it with a sigh of relief. The mental chatter, which caused him so much suffering, diminished.

■ □ ■

On the patio just outside the lobby, Sita Sofa had managed to settle her ample self into a droopy Honduras hammock. It was a rather treacherous thing to climb into, bobbing this way and that. At last, it accommodated her bulk, though any observer could see the hammock was under considerable strain.

Just a little toes-up before traipsing to my room with all this luggage, she thought.

On the same patio, partially hidden by a robust potted palm, Ivanta B. Alone was crouched in a nearby chair to better observe what she thought might be a Rapé alligator lizard that had darted under a hibiscus bush. She murmured, "Perhaps the gift shop will have a book on local flora and fauna that describes the species."

Hearing a voice, Sita, who had a knack for rambling on to whomever she could corner, began a soliloquy: "All things considered," she remarked in the general direction of the potted palm, "I've gotten through the ordeal of getting here rather well—decided to attend at the very last moment—just squeaked in before the deadline." She went on about the labors of packing—the assorted selection of pillows she'd brought, a few pounds of freeze-dried food, the water purifier. "You never know in these foreign places...." She droned on about her husband Herman, her weaving career and the variety of sturdy shoes she had packed. *After all, walking in sand could be precarious without a proper foundation.*

She didn't seem to notice that her audience, Ivanta, still absorbed in the lizard, hadn't murmured a word in reply.

As Sita settled deeper into the hammock, she drifted back in time to a painful childhood incident concerning a backyard swing that she'd not been allowed to play on. A long-buried rage surfaced, only to be subdued by another memory. "An old neighbor—Mable, yes, that was her name—had a hammock just like this one. Let's see, was it from Honduras or Ecuador? There were such bright red and green colors woven in. Or was it red and blue? Not that it matters...." Sita yawned as a wave of drowsiness overcame her.

■ □ ■

Jaw grimly set, C. King threw open the door to her *palapa*. As she did so, loose straw and dirt from the thatched roof sifted down onto her carefully arranged hair and immaculate black suit. She was beyond outrage, having struggled with her bags along an endless maze of sand paths. The porter who had offered to assist had looked a little too *native* for her taste.

Surveying her room with a practiced eye, she sniffed, "This will never do!" Still in her traveling attire, she threw herself into a cleaning frenzy, grabbing a hand towel from the bathroom and going over every surface to remove a film of thatched-roof dust. Though exhausted from her travels, she knew exactly how things must be for her to feel comfortable. Otherwise, she'd never manage to relax.

■ ▫ ■

Mona Preen drifted to the large window of her *palapa.* She had fluffed and hung her numerous outfits. They'd been thoughtfully chosen for maximum impact, though they appeared to be casually thrown together.

As she looked down at the beach and the shining sea beyond, her gaze came to rest on a man and woman, who were strolling arm-in-arm along the sand. She felt a sharp twinge of envy as she observed the intimate scene. The couple was obviously intoxicated with each other. Her heart contracted with the sudden painful remembrance of having been recently deserted by her last lover.

Why is it always like that for me, while others have all the luck? She gave herself over to the familiar inner lament and lowered herself onto the bed, taking care not to wrinkle her raw silk caftan.

A LITTLE BEFORE ONE-THIRTY P.M., the nine participants made their way to the meeting hall for Orientation. Filling the air with chatter, they entered the large domed room, collected and pressed on nametags, and settled into their places to await their first encounter with the famed Maya Llusion.

They didn't have long to wait. A deep, authoritative voice filled the room as a tall figure appeared. "Let us begin."

A gasp of awe was heard as the participants viewed the legendary teacher standing before them. She was swathed in multi-hued veils that floated and shifted, hypnotically engaging the attention of her audience.

"This is my first visit to the Ah So Retreat Center,

and isn't it a most intriguing spot?"

Each attendee, at this point, probably had a different definition of the word, *intriguing*, but they nodded
politely.

She went on, "We have a lot of material to cover
this afternoon, but let me begin by saying you are all
fortunate to have been given the privilege of attending
this retreat. You will most assuredly advance toward
your goal of spiritual growth, if you're willing to adhere
to my Principles and strictly follow my instructions."
She lifted her regal chin high. "I know from reviewing
your applications that most of you have been seeking
for a long time. But, in truth, you have only just be-
gun. Enlightenment comes only from a lifetime—
perhaps *many* lifetimes—of spiritual practice. Don't
imagine for a moment that it is easy. You must climb
the ladder of spiritual achievement with effort. Effort!
Effort!" Her voice escalated, bringing the group to stiff
attention.

She's exactly right, thought Govinda, nodding in
approval. *Nothing worth achieving has ever been
gained without intense work.* He found her sensational
to watch as she glided back and forth, veils undulat-

ing.

Maya continued, "Enlightenment must be earned. It is through years of meditation and self-discipline that you can purify your thoughts as well as your actions."

Thank God, I've already purified mine, thought C. King. *Too bad others haven't followed my example.*

"And the work is never done," Maya continued. "Spiritual knowledge must be continually expanded."

Hearing this, Ivanta perked up. She loved acquiring and cataloging any kind of knowledge. It gave her a feeling of security. *But what kind of price must I pay if I decide to align myself with such a demanding teacher?*

"The mind must be completely silenced," Maya went on, "so it is essential that you strengthen your concentration. It cannot waver. Unruly thoughts must be stamped out. And here is another important point: If you are progressing, you will find yourself able to control and negotiate your way through and beyond all unwanted situations by the sheer force of your personal will."

Mona leaned forward. *This is what I've yearned for—to no longer suffer or be haunted by my thoughts.*

The question is, can I believe this bizarre woman?

Maya continued. "Under my guidance, you will entertain, on a regular basis, extraordinary spiritual experiences and phenomena. These are signposts along the way, indicators of your progress. If you don't encounter them, you will simply have to work harder."

Wu Wu was thoroughly entranced. He had already chalked up an impressive list of 'spiritual experiences' and was eager to add more.

"I will teach you how to assess and judge the level of consciousness, both in yourself and others. This will allow you to remove yourself from lower vibrations that could hinder your own evolution." said Maya.

Perhaps I have come to the right place, after all, thought Pere. Then he noticed Maya's rather eerie, glittering eyes and he shuddered involuntarily. His mind immediately veered in an opposite direction. *Why in the world should I trust this woman?*

"We'll spend the rest of the afternoon going over my 'Seven Principles of Enlightenment' in some detail, so that you can know exactly where you stand on the spiritual ladder—*and,* perhaps just as important, so that you can know where others are. I've had these

Principles printed on handy cards, which you can easily carry with you for reference. If you need additional copies, I'd be happy to provide them, but I must ask that you not distribute copies to anyone who hasn't attended my courses. This is *very* powerful information, but in untrained hands, it could be, well, I'm sure you understand."

She handed the cards to Govinda and asked him to distribute them.

Betty Butterup wished she'd been chosen.

"Let's begin with Principle One," Maya said.

And for the next three hours, Maya Llusion lectured them on her prescription for enlightenment. By late afternoon, she had covered all the Principles. According to Maya, seekers must:

1. Have unquestioning allegiance to the master.
2. Have no other desires beyond the quest for spiritual attainment.
3. Have no attachments.
4. Become pure in thought, word and deed.
5. Maintain a still mind.
6. Be able to manifest higher states of conscious-

ness.

7. Completely rise above suffering and the entire human condition.

The sun had crept low in the sky as the Orientation session wore on. Most of the group, by now exhausted and completely overwhelmed, sat slumped in their chairs or fidgeted restlessly.

"I trust you all agree with these Principles," Maya said to the group. "Before we break for the day, I'd like to hear from each of you, in your own words, why you've come and what you hope to gain from this workshop."

The small audience stirred apprehensively, each wondering who would have the courage to speak first.

Bossisatva, who'd positioned himself front and center, decided to speak. Maya turned to his upraised hand. He took a deep breath, expanding his broad chest to fill even more space. "I am Baba Bossysatva," he announced, "and I'm here mostly to see whether you're as good as your propaganda. I'm also going to make certain you don't bullshit any of us. I've been listening very carefully, and I seriously doubt you have the ability to transfer spiritual power to us. I think your program is all smoke and mirrors. I know what I'm talking about because I've personally led dozens of workshops over the years." He crossed his arms over his massive chest and continued, "My tantric gatherings are extremely popular. I have a very large following." His threw Maya a challenging look.

Undaunted, Maya Llusion purred, "I doubt that you've heard of my recently created 'Tantric Tension Enhancing Ritual' I'm offering at this workshop." She dismissed Bossysatva with a detached stare and turned her attention to Mona Preen.

Mona sat in an artful pose of deep meditation, conveying she was already well along with Principle Number Five. She wore a nubby, grayish garment that she hoped would be recognized as the latest in environmentally correct fabrics. The material was made from recycled bicycle tires that suggested its wearer cared *very much* about the environment. It was a shame she'd been required to leave the unusual matching shoes at the door.

"Miss Preen!"

At the sound of her name, Mona fluttered open her

eyes. Everyone was looking at her, she realized with a start. She usually enjoyed such moments on center stage, but only if she'd prepared herself with both the proper inner attitude and outer image for the occasion. If she ever felt the subtle discomfort of her pretense, she rarely allowed herself to dwell on it. After all, the show must go on.

Shifting dramatically in her chair, she said, "Please, call me Mona. I must tell you I've had a very unhappy life. Now I'm devoutly seeking spiritual happiness." Her voice dropped to a stage whisper and her hands fluttered gracefully up to her heart. "The truth is, I've been abandoned many times in my life, and I'm simply too sensitive to experience any more loss. I'm counting on you, Maya, to help me be seen as worthy of the happiness enlightenment brings." She carefully adjusted the folds of her tread-mark-patterned scarf, which had slipped off her shoulder, and waited for the teacher's response.

Maya Llusion seemed to shimmer as she smiled down at Mona. "I'm *so* glad you're here," she said, with studied concern. "I want you to sign up for the mini-course tomorrow on 'Ancient Nubian Temple Rituals for Developing Your Image as a Uniquely Evolved, Spiritual Being.'"

Mona nodded doubtfully.

C. King sat stiffly on the rigid chair. So far, absolutely nothing pleased her, not the retreat center, not her companions—certainly an odd lot—and definitely not this intimidating workshop leader. They were all alien to her. Now she was being asked a question. She drew up her slender frame and focused intently on Maya Llusion. It was clearly the moment to set everyone straight. "I'm afraid I'm wasting my valuable time here." She addressed Maya Llusion defiantly. "I realize I'm here on earth with a very special mission—to become enlightened, to bring order and significance to life, and to create a transcendent state out of all this chaos." Her voice became slightly shrill. "I can't get on with my mission because of the confusion and lack of cooperation everywhere I turn." She stopped, immediately regretting her outburst.

With a swirl of veils, Maya Llusion rose to full height. Scowling down on C. King, she offered a solution: "You *definitely* need my mini-course, ' The Beginning Rituals for Removing Inner Chaos Through Intense Purification Practices.' "

Profoundly shocked, and feeling trivialized by what felt like an insult, a furious C. King grabbed her bag and, without a word, stormed from the room.

After the door slammed, Pere Anoiananda wanted to speak but hesitated. He had been listening to at least two sides of an intense, internal dialogue about the wisdom of speaking out to such a powerful authority figure. Finally, tentatively, he spoke. And once having given himself permission, there was no stopping him: "I'm not at all sure I belong here. I find your Principles utterly intimidating. What exactly is going to *happen?* It seems to me, the question, 'Why am I here?' has hidden meaning. It sounds like a trick question. How do I know that my answer won't be used against me? How do I know that I won't end up involved in some sort of craziness? Or even a cult!" He took a deep breath and visibly shuddered.

Maya Llusion smiled disdainfully at Pere, which sent him off on another tirade. "Here we are out in the middle of nowhere in a place teeming with aggressive insects and God only knows what else! I don't even know if this place has a doctor! I do know this climate is a breeding ground for botulism. I need a lot of answers and I need them soon! To think I paid good money for this!" Then he muttered, as a kind of afterthought or incantation, "I need something I can do to feel safe."

Maya Llusion swooped down, so that Pere feared he might be suffocated in her veils.

She said, "You can avoid fear by attending my training tomorrow called 'Psychic Dowsing for Bad Vibrations and Malevolent Entities.' Trust me," she added. "You *do* belong here."

Ivanta B. Alone had been the first to enter the meeting room, taking a seat in the last row of chairs. From here, she could unobtrusively observe the proceedings. She'd thought herself almost invisible and was startled when Maya Llusion's focus landed on her like a harsh spotlight.

"Why are you here, Ivanta?"

To Ivanta it seemed entirely too invasive to be asked why she was at the workshop, and she found she resented being exposed in so public a way. She'd prefer not to reveal why she'd come, beyond the research she planned into some of the underground caverns in the Tulum ruins. She might have stayed at a nearby hotel, but she'd been drawn here by a yearning for the protection she hoped enlightenment might bring. Ivanta had always felt vulnerable to life's intrusions. Now it seemed appalling to be intruded upon with such a personal question.

"Why am I here?" Ivanta repeated the question, buying time. When she spoke, it was as if from a great distance and in a slightly hushed voice. "Actually, I'm pursuing some obscure information concerning *cenotes*, the ancient underground caverns among the Tulum ruins. You might be interested to learn that *cenotes* were carved by a network of underground rivers and may have been used as initiation chambers by Mayan priests many centuries ago." Then she added, to distance herself from Maya Llusion, "Now, I realize that my studies are much more important than anything that's being offered here. So you probably won't be seeing very much of me."

The realization that someone in the workshop knew about *cenotes* and their hidden power caused a ripple of apprehension in Maya. "It's entirely appropriate that you're here," Maya countered coolly. "However, without guidance, probing into the ancient secrets of this area can be dangerous."

Intrigued, but not wanting to show it, Ivanta folded her arms and retreated into herself.

Maya next focused on Sita Sofa, who was off on a memory trip, reminiscing about how the clerk, Eduardo, reminded her of Julio—was that his name? Maybe it was Martino?—her Latin lover of fifteen years ago, back when she was living in Berkeley. She recalled the apartment they'd shared with the awful plumbing. She'd worked on the tub faucet and the parts had fallen down the drain, never to be found again. It was so....

Suddenly, startled from her reverie by the sound of Maya Llusion's penetrating voice, Sita sat up straight, eyes wide.

"Please introduce yourself and give us your reason for being here."

"I'm Sita," she said. She attempted to focus on the scene at hand but an entirely new story snagged her attention. "I'm here because of Kitty Doyle who I ran into at the Wonder Weavers convention last fall. She was just back from the Ah So Retreat Center. She said it was such a relaxing place. You must have heard of Kitty. She's been weaving since '68. Her work is everywhere. I knew her in Berkeley years ago. She sold me my first loom. Have you ever seen the way those old looms are built? Much better than anything you can find on the market today."

"Sita, could we have a clear answer from you? Why are you here?" Maya Llusion's commanding voice sought to draw Sita back to the present.

A familiar feeling of resistance washed over Sita: Somebody wanted something from her and there was no way that she was going to be made to comply. An insincere smile broke over her face, followed by a false laugh. "Guess I'm here to find peace and quiet." *Anything to get you off my back*, was her inner thought.

"I have the perfect assignment for you," said Maya. "It will bring you out of your confused condition and help you with Principle Five. You will take my course tomorrow on 'How to Stop the Mind.' The electrodes placed on the head are practically painless." She gave Sita a disdainful look which Sita avoided by rummaging through a bulging, hand-woven carpetbag. Trail mix, eye shades and two sets of ear plugs spilled out, and there was a moment of confusion as those nearby scrambled to retrieve them.

It was Betty Butterup's turn to speak next. She smiled engagingly at Maya Llusion, "I know what I really want," she said in her sweetest voice. "I want to serve where I can do the greatest good. You are such an amazing and influential teacher, and you're making such a difference in the world." Betty's cornflower blue eyes entreated. "Maybe I could be of some help to you. Do you need a personal assistant, or...? I'm also a massage therapist."

With a look of disgust, Bossy thought, *What bullshit!*

"Of course, my dear," replied Maya unctuously. "I'll speak with you after the meeting. You could start by pressing my veils."

Betty nodded, pleased. Now she would be taken into the inner circle. She tried not to notice the uncomfortable suspicion that she'd do almost anything to make herself indispensable.

Wu Wu Way's hand shot up. He realized that Maya Llusion's Principles were radical, but still he felt a buzz of excitement when he thought of all the possibilities awaiting him this weekend. He spoke with great enthusiasm. "I'm Wu Wu Way, and my purpose in being here is to expand this already wonderful feeling I have of being enlightened. I *absolutely know* I'm a special conduit for the Cosmic Plan. But after hearing your approach to enlightenment, I have to question whether we could co-create together. My latest idea is to use bungee jumping to increase *chi* in the elderly. As a matter of fact, I'm off to speak to a convention of notable gerontologists immediately after this workshop." He pushed his rose tinted-glasses up on his nose.

"You've certainly come to the right place, Wu Wu," Maya said. "I have a special assignment for you—the examination and evaluation of all your past life lessons to qualify for the once-in-a-lifetime, 'Accelerated Enlightenment Program' that I'm offering to just a few very special students."

Wu Wu sat back, pleased and a bit overwhelmed, and surreptitiously pressed the button to activate his Vibro-Life Pleasure Device that he'd strapped around his waist beneath his Nehru jacket.

From the first sentence of his introduction, Govinda Go Go projected a cool efficiency. He informed

Maya Llusion, "I'm a multi-level marketing entrepreneur. I hope it doesn't seem immodest if I tell you that, in less than a year, I've had tremendous success with this. I've been pursuing higher consciousness hoping it would support that success. Also, Maya, I brought along my latest product for you to see. I know you'll want to include it in your workshops." He continued speaking rapidly to prevent interruption, regaling his audience with his ambitious plans.

Maya beamed. "But surely a successful man of the world doesn't need my help?"

For a fleeting moment, Govinda felt a hollowness deep within that his success had failed to fill. He avoided this empty feeling by gathering his 'successful identity' like a cloak around him. He looked her squarely in the eye and said, "I'm always open to new ideas to enhance my spiritual work, although I find yours pretty extreme."

She gave him a long, piercing look and suggested he attend her mini-course on "Mastering the Technique of Packaging Yourself as a Successful Spiritual Seeker."

When the questioning ended, Maya Llusion fixed

each of the nine in turn with a mesmerizing gaze. "Remember," she said, in what could be taken as a threatening tone, "You can, in time, become enlightened, but you must do everything I ask of you. We will meet again at nine A.M. tomorrow." Then all at once she was gone.

An enormous feeling of unease had settled over the group. Something odd and unnerving was going on. A few wondered whether they were selling their souls. The seekers filed out silently, each ruminating on his own thoughts.

Maya llusion slipped out of the meeting hall, carefully preserving her aura of infallibility as she made her way to her remote *palapa* at the cliff's edge. When she closed the door, however, her demeanor changed, mirroring her shift in mood. Feeling uneasy and drained, she slowly lowered herself into a large wicker chair by the window and let out a deep sigh.

Despite her best efforts, depressing thoughts overtook her. *What is happening? Why am I not commanding the respect I once did?*

It must be the caliber of the students, she decided, feeling momentarily comforted. *They are much more independent than my students used to be, and none of them has what it takes. It's a long, difficult road to enlightenment, however I'm an exceptional teacher and I'm always willing to do whatever it takes to lift them up out of their ignorance and powerlessness.*

Perhaps it was the word, 'powerlessness,' that triggered the rush of uninvited memories from her dismal childhood. As Maya tried to push them away, an old feeling of helplessness came over her. Pictures of the past flooded in—the desperate poverty, her mother struggling each day to make ends meet, her father dying a long, slow death. Once again she felt their anguish and her own inability as a child to change any of it. She remembered her vow to herself to *never* feel trapped or powerless again.

"I was right to want to escape and create a more dynamic life," she exclaimed aloud as she tried to shake herself free of painful feelings, feelings that she *never* permitted herself to entertain. *It's this place. There is a strange energy here.* She shuddered, remembering the unnerving sensation yesterday when she arrived and walked over to the ruins, when she felt she'd lost her boundaries.

Maya sat for some time staring out at the horizon. Falling into a timeless trance, she felt transported back to the ashram in India. Scenes of her life there with Guru Pushiji began to roll by like a film before her eyes, each scene vividly relived. She saw herself as the young woman she had been, seated before her teacher, so eager to embrace all the required practices and austerities.

I did everything required of me, she realized, flushing with pride. *It was so difficult, but all through the years, I never faltered. I sacrificed, gave up all physical comforts, meditated long hours with my body aching and my mind on fire. I laid all my desires before the altar of spiritual purification. And at last, I was rewarded.*

Now, sitting in her *palapa,* she remembered the dynamic turning point in her life as though it were yesterday. She had been meditating for many months in a remote Himalayan cave when her sense of reality suddenly shifted, revealing a glimpse of Oneness. In the ensuing clarity, 'Maya' didn't exist any longer. Yet awareness infused everything. At first, this revelation was blissful, but gradually the glimpse of truth faded and personal identity reasserted itself. *I am enlightened,* she decided, and immediately experienced a satisfying sense of accomplishment for having risen above the human condition. She felt in control of her life and wanted nothing more to do with the vast reality she had earlier glimpsed, knowing it would threaten her feeling of power and authority.

Maya had left India soon after to begin her career as a spiritual teacher. She consciously developed a mystique, an elusiveness that in her mind elevated her in stature. She designed rigorous and innovative programs to attract the most enthusiastic seekers. As her fame grew, Maya relished the adoration and the feeling of being special and wise.

But now, at every turn, she was reminded of her need to reinvent herself as a forceful presence on the spiritual stage. After years of success, it was appalling to be faced with this necessity. Maya secretly hoped to enhance her status by obtaining ancient secrets for amassing power which were rumored to be hidden in the Tulum ruins. She alone knew that this was her real reason for coming to Tulum.

Maya sat motionless for a while. Through the window, she saw that darkness was falling.

A LAZY GOLDEN HAZE enveloped the grounds of the Ah So Retreat Center. But, however relaxing, the glow of the setting sun did little to relieve the agitation of the seekers as they made their way along the path to the open air bar and dining room.

At the bar, Wu Wu Way and Baba Bossysatva had already achieved an advanced cocktail hour shimmer. The bartender spoke little English, but that hadn't slowed them down. Extensive arm waving and pointing had brought the desired results and, now fortified by colorful exotic beverages, they appeared to be best of friends.

Betty Butterup entered and sidled up to the two men, looking rather limp from an extended session with a hot iron. "What are you drinking, Wu Wu?"

"I have no idea," he said, as Betty perched herself

on the barstool next to him. After a series of flamboyant gestures, he procured for her a vicious looking purple drink shaded by a miniature orange umbrella. "I think this one's called a Titanic."

C. King slid onto a stool, saying to no one in particular, "Can't make any sense of this drink menu. I don't usually drink." Bossy immediately took charge and ordered her a large Boomerang. Still harboring uncomfortable feelings of guilt for having stormed out of the Orientation, C. King tentatively asked, "What do you think of Maya Llusion?"

"Not very damn much," Bossy replied. "She needs watching. She's not what she seems. I'm not going to hand over my power to her, that's for sure."

This prompted a large gulp from C. King, whose Boomerang was rapidly disappearing. She too was uneasy about Maya Llusion's approach to spiritual freedom. Maya had said things that went against her own strong sense of right and wrong, leaving her disturbed and provoked. She needed to sort things out, or set things straight, but she didn't know how. Today's events were a reflection of every area of her life. It all felt familiar yet somehow wrong.

Suddenly, a medley of voices increased the noise level in the bar. Govinda Go Go, Mona Preen and Pere Anoiananda arrived. Mona looked disturbed and Govinda had his arm around her waist. He'd obviously been doing some hands-on comforting.

Pere Anoiananda slipped onto an empty bar stool, preparing to drown his agitation. Somehow he was drawn to a libation called a Scorpion. Ivanta appeared and in precise Spanish ordered a Torpedo.

Betty simply could not contain her annoyance a moment longer. "I feel *used!* Maya put me in a small, hot room—a closet really—with no windows and handed me an enormous pile of those *draperies* she wears, pointed to the iron and left me there all alone. It was humiliating. She wasn't even gracious enough to say thank you. Didn't give me so much as a nod. The least she could do to show a little gratitude would be to invite me for a private chat." She finished defiantly, "I am *not* her slave!"

"Have I missed Happy Hour?" chirped a voice. Sita crowded in to order a drink. With Ivanta's help, she ordered a dangerous looking chartreuse concoction and began describing her recent beach adventure, which was no adventure in any real sense, just a report on how she'd spent an hour after the meeting. She droned on about California not allowing trash on its beaches, the hardness of the beach chairs, and some nosy man she'd met. "He said he was some kind of a detective—wouldn't think you would need them here, so rural and all. Of course, there are all types of tourists at the ruins—must see those before I leave. A funny little man, very curious about this place. Lots of questions."

The last caught Bossy's attention. "What did you tell him?" he asked.

"Couldn't tell him much, could I?" she replied. "I did say I was a bit let down after our first meeting. Found her—the leader—to be very strange, theatrical and demanding. Wish I hadn't come so far. However, the hammocks are pleasant."

C. King, who had been listening intently, snorted into her empty glass and ordered another drink. "I knew it," she said in a slightly slurred voice. "I felt it from the beginning, something very odd about Maya Llusion."

Pere had been in a dilemma for hours, fighting

dark battles in his head about what to do: *Should I stay? Should I go? I don't feel safe in the presence of Maya Llusion.* At least he knew that much. "I don't think she has the power she claims to have," he declared and went back to contemplating his Scorpion.

With an exasperated sigh, Mona said, "I really don't feel this workshop meets my needs. The course that Maya suggested I attend tomorrow couldn't possibly change the dissatisfaction I feel." She spoke passionately, a flush mounting on her cheeks. "I've investigated things like she suggested before and they never work—or they only work for a little while."

Betty, sitting next to her, turned and said, "You aren't alone. I imagine we're all feeling disappointed. Being used by Maya has jolted me into seeing how I overextend myself."

Mona was clearly touched by this gesture of friendship. Prompted by Betty's attention, she whispered, "I'm just beginning to realize that I've never felt authentic inside. Sometimes I feel like an actress in a play."

Betty sympathetically leaned toward Mona. "We should talk later. Maybe I can help," she said, secretly reveling in the importance of feeling needed.

Ivanta sat at the end of the bar with her reference book on the Tulum ruins, engrossed in the section on *cenotes*.

Pere sat next to Ivanta, morbidly nursing his drink. His inner turmoil erupted once again and he interrupted her concentration. "I think she's rather sinister, don't you?"

"Who?" demanded Ivanta, obviously exasperated at being bothered by this twitchy little man. Actually, she had been half-listening to the group's conversation. She just didn't want them to know it.

"Maya Llusion—*sinister!*" Pere repeated loudly.

"More likely, she simply has an immense ego and believes she's exceptionally important," Ivanta said and turned back to her book dismissively.

■ □ ■

Inspector Hidalgo Neti Neti sat at a small table quite close to the group at the bar, and Sergeant Salvadore Shadow ambled in to join him. The sergeant slumped into a chair, bumping the table with his knees and sloshing his boss's drink.

"Sorry, sir," Shadow said and ordered a beer.

The inspector had been eavesdropping on the conversation at the bar, and the word "sinister" had caught his attention. *An odd assortment of people*, he thought, as he assessed them with a practiced eye. "They look disgruntled, don't they?" he remarked to Sergeant Shadow.

Shadow wiped beer foam from his droopy mustache with the back of his cuff. "Yes, yes, very upset, sir." He was enjoying this rare evening out and wanted nothing remotely resembling a disagreement to spoil it.

Neti Neti said in a low voice, "I'd like to know who this Maya person is. She definitely appears to be up to no good."

The group of nine were too absorbed in their discontent and their exotic drinks to notice they were being watched by the Mexican police—or that they had caught the interest of a tall, Mayan man seated alone in a corner. He was, in fact, a shaman called Quantomundi, well-known to the indigenous people of the area.

Inspector Neti Neti did notice Quantomundi's presence, however, and he was curious as to what might have brought this shaman out to the bar at the Ah So Retreat Center.

QUANTOMUNDI'S CALLING TO SPIRITUALITY had come about in a most unusual way. When Quantomundi was a boy, his grandfather, a shaman himself, had looked for indications that his grandson would be the next bearer of the tradition. He had used shamanic tools, among them divination, dream interpretation and appeals to the spirits of other dimensions, to obtain verification of this; but none of the usual signs appeared. However, he never gave up hope and through the years stood by as a guide for the growing boy.

A laughing, happy child who seemed to enjoy whatever the moment held, Miguel, as he was called then, displayed none of the traits of a potential shaman. Miguel was fifteen when his sunny, carefree disposition was suddenly smothered by a depression that came from out of nowhere. He began to ask deep, searching questions, to which he had no answers: "Who am I?" "Why am I here?" "Why am I so unhappy?" He recognized his grandfather's desire for him to continue the lineage, but Miguel had no inclination to fulfill this expectation. He was allowed to observe many of the shamanic practices and rituals and felt there was something missing for him in that tradition, which troubled him greatly.

The future seemed bleak to Miguel. A great emptiness engulfed him, which he seemed incapable of shaking off. He often left the house, wandering off by himself without a word to anyone.

One overcast morning, Miguel left home early, unseen by his grandfather. Heavy storm clouds gathered. Ignoring them, Miguel headed for the Tulum ruins, a favorite place of solace for him during these tormented days. He would often sit for hours behind a large rock outcropping, retreating from the world to sort through dark thoughts which held him in their grip.

That day, as he approached the ruins, the tropical storm hit full-force. Blinded by torrential rain, he became disoriented and confused. He moved unsteadily across the uneven ground, frantically searching for some familiar landmark. Without warning, he stumbled, felt his feet give way, and tumbled heavily into dark oblivion.

When Miguel came to and opened his eyes, he saw only a faint light that seemed to come from somewhere above him. *Where am I? Have I died?* He inhaled deeply and a earthy smell filled his nostrils. As he tried to get up from the cold, damp surface, a sharp pain tore down his left leg into his ankle. An icy fear gripped him as he realized his helplessness.

Miguel lay on the floor of the cavern in the grip of a fear so great it took his breath away. Finally, he summoned the energy to call out for help, but his voice only echoed back at him. Gradually, his eyes became more accustomed to the darkness and he formed a sense of the space around him. That was when he realized he had probably fallen into one of the hidden underground chambers in the ruins—a *cenote*.

Several times Miguel tried to move, but each time he did, the pain was excruciating. *No one knows where I am. I could die here!* A new wave of terror engulfed him. He reviewed his brief life—the early joy that had turned to depression, regret at not fulfilling his grandfather's dream for him. Hot tears of shame and anger brimmed and ran down his cheeks. A shudder of grief shook his body, triggering more pain from his injury. Lying there, trapped and helpless, Miguel experienced a rush of thoughts that arose to parade through his mind. Then, after what seemed like many hours, it began to dawn on him that he was something more than his troubled mind and feelings; he was also the *observer* of them. As he watched his thoughts, they began to lose their power over him. The experience reminded him of movies he'd seen with his grandfather at the theater in Tulum, where events appeared real but were actually all make-believe. *Then, if I am not my thoughts, who am I? What is real?*

Here in the darkness, stripped of all irrelevancies and distractions, Miguel's urgent questions yielded up a startling clarity—like the light of the sun emerging from a total solar eclipse. The heavy veil of fear, confusion and doubt dissolved and with it Miguel's sense of *me* disappeared. Where Miguel had thought himself a *somebody,* defined by his mind and body, he now recognized himself as *present awareness*, vibrantly alive and awake and outside any context or constraint of time. This awareness was so pervasive and familiar, it had been overlooked entirely, perhaps because of the mind's fascination with drama.

Now, illuminated by the light of awareness, all of life was seen as unconditional love celebrating itself in all its diversity. It was a profound, life-changing moment.

"Miguel!" He heard the muffled call of his grandfather's voice, "Miguel!"

During Miguel's recovery, Grandfather realized that his grandson had experienced a total shift in consciousness. He had left the identity of Miguel behind. Grandfather renamed his grandson Quantomundi.

Now, years later, as Quantomundi observed the group at the bar, he understood that their suffering was due to misidentification. They had forgotten their true nature and believed that they *were* the characters they were playing on the world stage. He also realized that this group had the potential to hear the truth. He would continue to watch and listen and perhaps approach them after dinner.

As the full moon rose to cast a silver path across the calm sea, Govinda announced, "Time for dinner." He had been watching as the waiters set the tables at the nearby, open-air dining room. The group moved to the dining area, more than ready for the diversion of food.

"Guess we're stuck together for the weekend," said Sita, delighted to retain her captive audience. But even she had lost some of her conversational stamina as she attended to her inner ruminations on Maya Llusion.

They were placed at a large round table. Bossy was the only one who noticed that the wiry, little man and the tall fat one had left the bar and were once again seated within hearing distance. *Maybe that's the detec-*

*tive Sita talked to on the beach, along with his sidekick.
I wonder what they're doing here?*

Between courses, C. King turned to Govinda and asked him to explain his multi-level product to her. It didn't take much prompting. "Its called Expando," he said in a voice meant to engage the entire table. "It's a series of tapes that play sounds in a range of vibrations that accelerate enlightenment."

That drew Wu Wu's attention. "Are drugs involved?"

"Nope. Strictly on the up-and-up," Govinda replied. "It *is* the latest craze, at least among spiritual seekers, because it produces an instant high."

"Is it addictive?" C. King asked in a critical tone. Not waiting for an answer, she pursued, "And if it's so easy, then why are you here?"

Govinda smiled tolerantly, covering the second wave of emptiness to hit him that day. He quickly rallied. "I'm really only here to promote my product with the hope that Maya Llusion will start to use it in her workshops. I thought I made that clear this afternoon." He turned slightly to give her a good view of his handsome and, he hoped, confident profile.

Meanwhile, at a nearby table, Inspector Neti Neti had caught the word 'drugs.' Immediately on red alert, he strained to hear details and picked up 'instant high' and 'addicted.' His suspicions were confirmed. "This definitely calls for further investigation. We'll prowl the grounds tonight, see what we turn up."

Shadow, happily absorbed in his free dinner, nodded in agreement.

At the round table, Wu Wu carefully laid down his fork and said to no one in particular, "I'm looking forward to tomorrow. After this afternoon, it'll be fascinating to see how Maya Llusion works with us."

"I find it quite astonishing that you haven't seen more than enough already," commented Ivanta. "No human being could possibly master her Seven Principles. She's a charlatan if I ever saw one, and we'd be well-advised to ask for our money back." She ended this unaccustomed outburst with a short brittle laugh.

Sita, bibbed and ardently stuffing herself on lobster, stopped chewing a moment to address Ivanta. "Tell us about those *cenotes* you've been studying."

Ivanta lacked the temperament for exhibitionism. She spoke *only* when firmly in control of all the facts and never risked making a fool of herself. So it was not surprising that she took a rather dim view of Sita's question. "I'm not really prepared to speak about *cenotes*, not until I gather more data."

"Okay," Sita said. "Well, they sound interesting," and turned back to her lobster.

With a visionary glimmer in his eyes, Wu Wu said, "I'm certainly going to get something out of this weekend. In fact, I intend to get what I came for."

"And what's that?" Pere inquired.

Wu Wu looked slightly bewildered and, for a split second, a feeling of weariness washed over him. He was so tired of maintaining an enlightened image, but he swiftly roused himself and replied, "I want more bliss. One can never have enough bliss! I imagine it's part of Maya Llusion's plan to take us to the ancient ruins to improve our chances for spiritual growth and help us with the Seven Principles. I believe she was a High Priestess in a past life and has returned to Tulum to further enhance her mystical powers."

"What an idiotic suggestion," Bossy laughed with a look that would wilt Medusa's hair. "High Priestess, my ass! Get your feet on the ground, man."

Betty, who had been ready to support Wu Wu's fantasy, bit her tongue.

Mona said despondently, "Well, she certainly hasn't lived up to her reputation so far, and I can't imagine those mini-workshops she's assigning are going to make this weekend memorable."

"I'm having second thoughts about going to that demeaning course on purification practices that she assigned me," C. King said. "And have any of you wondered how she'll facilitate so many courses by herself?"

"Oh, I'm sure she has help," stated Betty, not sure of anything at this point but wanting to portray herself as an insider.

"She certainly made it clear that she was going to assist me," said Govinda defiantly.

"She indicated the same to me," echoed Wu Wu.

"Really?" said Bossy. "I didn't hear any promises."

"How did she get to be such a renowned teacher if so little is known about her methods?" Pere asked, still attempting to figure out Maya's motives. He desperately wanted resolution so that one side of his internal argument could win. He hated the paralyzing sense of being lost in a quagmire of confusion.

"A teacher can be very clever at this spiritual game," answered Bossy. He had no intention of exposing his own brand of craftiness, but he spoke with authority.

This statement only served to underline Pere's fears.

"Tomorrow should be interesting to watch," mused Ivanta.

"But aren't you going to participate?" Betty queried. "I think that we should all at least try to be open and willing."

Sita nodded approval and tucked into a flan dripping with caramel sauce.

Ivanta answered Betty, "I *will* attempt to get information about the *cenotes* out of her."

"Look, follow my lead tomorrow," Bossy said, "I'll make sure you're all taken care of. Just don't be threatened or cajoled into offering her your allegiance. You noticed that's her first Principle, *allegiance*."

Mona said, "Those Seven Principles are over the top, like Ivanta said."

"Let's wait and see," said Wu Wu, not wanting to end the evening on a down note.

The group rose and moved toward the door. Neti Neti watched them leave, his long bloodhound nose twitching in anticipation of some long overdue sleuthing. He stood up, his chin jutting eagerly, and made for the door. Sergeant Shadow followed.

The shaman, in his dark corner, reconsidered approaching the group. *They're not quite ready. I will wait.*

Outside, C. King noticed the wind was up and dark clouds were racing across the moon.

Walking beside her, Wu Wu said, "Looks like we might be in for one of those infamous tropical storms."

C. King shuddered, remembering her *palapa's* insubstantial roof.

Pere, announcing he was heading for the Office for a can of bug spray, bid everyone goodnight.

Betty moved forward and positioned herself in Wu Wu's path. Thrusting her newly acquired bosom at him, she struck an inviting pose. Wu Wu pretended not to notice and turned toward his *palapa*.

Betty pouted briefly, thinking she must have failed to master some vital procedure in the "Discovering the Barbie Within" workshop. But she recovered quickly and turned to Mona, who was standing behind her. "Remember we were going to have a chat?"

Mona, eager to be distracted from her ever-growing feeling of despair, followed Betty to her room. Once inside the *palapa,* Mona draped her willowy frame onto one of the large wicker chairs facing the windows and sighed. Betty poured two glasses of sparkling water and sank into a matching chair. They could hear the storm approaching.

Betty asked, "What drew you into spiritual seeking, Mona? You seem so *together.*"

Mona was silent for a moment, uncertain where to begin. Then she uttered one truthful word: "Depression. I feel like I'm fatally flawed—a mistake or something. I never seem to be able to let myself be happy. Or let myself *be.*" She immediately felt ashamed of the admission.

However unrealistic, Betty wanted to believe she had the ability to pull Mona out of what was probably a lifelong depression. "So you thought spiritual seeking would ease your suffering?"

"Well, not the *seeking,* but the *finding,*" answered Mona. "Except the finding hasn't happened. That's why I counted so heavily on Maya Llusion. Now I feel pretty hopeless about her help in finding inner peace. I've had so many teachers. I even went to India and almost died there—had several near collisions on those narrow Himalayan roads and then the dysentery...." Her voice trailed off, her body drooping in an aura of fragility and tragedy.

"What would you need from Maya Llusion tomorrow to make this workshop a success?" Betty asked, finally admitting to herself that she was in over her head.

"A miracle," whispered Mona. For a brief moment, she clearly recognized herself playing a part—and playing it very well—in the story called "Mona and Her Sad, Unfulfilled Life." Jolted, she turned the focus away from herself. "What about you? What turned you into a spiritual seeker?"

Betty stared blankly. She had been so intent on Mona's story that she had to stop and try to find herself. This was not an unfamiliar feeling. Hesitantly, she said, "I don't know really—guess I'm still looking for love and approval. I also had a teacher and was totally devoted to him. I served him day and *night*—emphasis on 'night.' But just like Maya and the ironing, I ended up feeling used." A wave of repulsion swept through her as she thought, *I hate it when I sell myself for approval.*

As sheets of rain began pelting the windows, Mona said, "I'd best be off before the storm gets worse." She rose with a wistful smile, still aware of being an actress as she delivered her last line: "I hope I didn't burden you too much with my troubles."

"That's okay," Betty replied absently.

"Thank you," Mona said, leaning forward for a brief hug before she slipped out the door.

Hurrying through the wind and rain, Mona began worrying about Retreadalon, the recycled bicycle tire material of her dress and shoes, and how it would respond to the drenching rain. The labels had definitely instructed, 'Dry Clean Only.' Once inside her room, she realized that she was emitting a distinctly rubbery aroma.

■ □ ■

Sita, who had stopped by the Office for an armload of extra blankets, was also caught in the downpour. As she hurried to her *palapa*, she wondered what all the fuss at dinner had been about. True, she wasn't especially impressed with Maya Llusion, but the meal had been excellent and the retreat center was magnificent. Safely back in her *palapa*, she draped the sodden blankets over various chairs and a table. She'd sort through her feelings tomorrow.

■ □ ■

C. King walked with Bossysatva toward their rooms. Even if others thought Bossy was arrogant, she liked his unreserved outspoken behavior. Although she hated to admit it, she also appreciated his virile masculinity. The attraction made her uncomfortable and slightly embarrassed, especially given their difference in age.

Just as the rain began, she bid Bossy goodnight and entered her room. *Things used to be so simple, didn't they? So orderly and predictably gratifying.* She poured herself a neat scotch from the secret flask she traveled with and sat down to ponder her dilemma. It had been an appalling day and there was no hope that tomorrow would bring any relief. She had come here because she found it increasingly difficult to subdue her inner rage. It erupted often and at inopportune times—like today when she'd stormed out of the afternoon session. Such behavior simply did not fit her image of a spiritually evolved person. But she could *not*, no, she simply could *not*, place herself in Maya Llusion's hands, not if it meant being humiliated in front of the group. Still, she was not a quitter. She had invested too many years in seeking to stop now.

Without warning, a voice in her head demanded, *What exactly are you seeking?* Maya's question echoed: *Why are you here?* For once, her mind didn't rush to answer. She waited for her heart to speak. *I want to feel all right about myself, to know that everything's all right just as it is, and that there's nothing I need to fix.*

NETI NETI AND SHADOW DIVIDED the list of suspects between them and set off to find evidence of wrong-doing.

Sergeant Shadow's first assignment was to check out Pere Anoiananda's *palapa*. When he arrived there, he found it dark and unoccupied. *Might as well slip in and snoop around,* decided Shadow, as he deftly picked the lock. He had no sooner shut the door behind him when he heard footsteps on the path. Panicked, Shadow lurched into the shower, closing the white plastic curtain to conceal his mammoth frame. He held his breath as he heard the front door open and click shut. Shifting slightly, he bumped against the faucet, which produced a stream of icy water. Startled and drenched, he tore out of the shower, hopelessly tangled in the curtain.

Pere, watching this apparition streak past, concluded it was a ghost and attempted to immobilize it with a squirt of bug spray.

■ □ ■

Meanwhile, Neti Neti crept through the wind and rain to an uncurtained window. He crouched below the sill and gradually raised his head. The rain streaming off his hat made visibility difficult but not impossible. Inside the *palapa*, Betty was admiring her bare, remodeled breasts in an effort to regain her confidence following Wu Wu's rejection. She inflated her chest, looked in the mirror, and saw eyes looking back at her from the window. She screamed and ran to the light switch, then shaking with fright, groped her way to the bed and dove under the covers.

■ □ ■

Having successfully avoided Betty, Wu Wu entered the sanctity of his room and prepared for bed by lighting indigo candles and a stick of hemp incense. The candles were part of a nightly ritual to open his third eye while he slept, and the incense should, he hoped, induce fifth dimensional dreaming.

■ □ ■

Soaked and discouraged, Neti Neti was still on the prowl. And however chastened he felt by the Peeping Tom episode—he knew he had lingered overly long at Betty's window—he still hadn't lost the manic, crime-stopping glint in his eye. He sniffed expertly outside Wu Wu's *palapa*. "Ah ha," he said, "marijuana!" Deliriously encouraged by this sensory input, he hurried off to find Sergeant Shadow.

■ □ ■

After the apparition streaked from his room, Pere sat down abruptly—to keep from collapsing. *What was that?* He sat in the dark without moving or thinking. Time stopped, and with it came the cessation of his thoughts. Yet, even without thoughts or a sense of time, it was apparent that *he* was still here, or *something* was, something that was aware yet completely still. It felt familiar—and not at all frightening. Then he dismissed it—*I'm shocked, stunned. That's all.*

He got up, took his flashlight and went out into the storm, making his way through near-horizontal sheets of rain to Bossysatva's thatched hut. Seeing no lights, Pere assumed Bossy had retired for the night but, in desperation, knocked anyway.

Bossy threw the door open and pointed the strong beam of a flashlight into Pere's eyes. "Oh, sorry. Damned lights went out. Come in." He pulled the dripping Pere in and shut the door against the storm.

As they placed their flashlights on a table, Bossy remarked, "You look like you've seen a ghost."

"That's exactly what I've seen," Pere sputtered. "It's voodoo. This place is haunted!"

"Come on, man, I know you're out of your element here but that's taking it a little far. What exactly did you see?"

"As I entered my room, something very large and white streaked past me in the dark. It practically knocked me down!"

"She's up to something—I know it," Bossy stated emphatically.

"Who?" croaked Pere.

"Who? Maya Llusion, of course! She's attempting to terrify us into compliance to go along with her program."

"But why?" asked Pere, still clinging to his voodoo theory. And then, even in this dire moment, he had a glimmer of the bizarre cosmic joke that had brought him to this unlikely place in search of inner peace.

Bossy, who could be unexpectedly kindhearted when he wasn't feeling threatened, offered Pere his sofa and a blanket.

■ □ ■

Meanwhile, Sita had just nestled in bed, without enough blankets, to watch a TV talk show in Spanish. She didn't understand a word but that hardly mattered. When the electricity failed, she turned over and began to muse about the day. She felt uncomfortably stirred up. She wished the eight other participants weren't quite so intense, nor Maya so invasive and heavy-handed. She had enjoyed being an armchair seeker for so long, she actually shuddered at the prospect of any real internal change. Turning from these disturbing thoughts, she drew the bedspread over her head and was soon fast asleep.

■ □ ■

Govinda arrived at his room just as the storm broke. He'd grown impatient as the dinner dragged on, having planned a long evening of satisfying work in his portable office.

Well, I can put in a few hours before sleep. As he changed into pajamas, he reflected on his encounter that afternoon with Maya Llusion. Despite all the turbulence around him, he thought it had gone rather well. *As a matter of fact, I'm certain I impressed her.* The only off-note had been that altogether too-elementary self-marketing program she'd suggested. But he was certain that, when she realized his potential, he'd be immediately placed in a more appropriate training. After all, much of his worldly success had come from his ability to sell an image. *And at least I'll be doing something besides sitting around all day in some pointless meditation. That kind of enforced idleness is pure hell.*

Before turning on the computer, he placed by his bed the manual for the speed-reading course he was taking, along with his current for-pleasure book, *How to Work While You Sleep.*

Outside, the storm raged. When the power failed and all the lights went out, Govinda sat down on the bed, trying to subdue an increasing sense of unease. *My God, I can't work in the dark. What'll I do?* He resisted the urge to return to the bar through the violent storm. Their electricity would probably be out, too. It came as a bit of a shock to realize the intensity of his addiction to work. He felt quite empty and worthless without it. Uncomfortable feelings arose and pulled him into despair. Curling up beneath his blankets, he tried to think positive thoughts. Then, appalled to find himself in this condition, he wondered, *What is it about this place that seems to exaggerate everything?*

ACT II

SOMETIME IN THE NIGHT the storm blew over, bringing a morning that was glorious with crystal clear air and a glittering sea. The Ah So Retreat Center's gardeners were out early working on the grounds, cleaning up palm fronds and debris from the storm.

Ivanta sat alone at breakfast. An early riser, she had already enjoyed a dip in the ocean, and now, strong coffee and a frugal Continental breakfast were reaffirming her appreciation of life.

It had been a rough night. She had been studying up on *cenotes*, with an uncanny feeling that she was being watched, when the electricity failed. Then she'd lain awake for hours reviewing the day and had finally come face-to-face with her disappointment. For, although it was true she was interested in *cenotes*, she'd really come to the Ah So Retreat Center for expanded consciousness. In the dark, chilled room, she realized that this was a very unlikely place to find it. Uninvited feelings of loneliness washed over her, and she felt keenly the isolation that her jealously guarded privacy always brought on. She vanquished these feelings by determinedly focusing on the next day and how she might avoid Maya Llusion's prying.

Sleep finally came, bringing a nightmare about a frantic attempt to escape from a land of loveless robots. Horrified, she woke up and was shocked by the sudden realization that her waking life was also a dream. The awareness was too startling and fleeting to hang onto, but there was no denying that she had seen it clearly, for an instant.

■ □ ■

At dawn, C. King awoke with a groan. The raging storm had kept her tossing and turning most of the night, and now sleep would not return, not in this place under these conditions. Everything was chaotic.

She looked up and saw a pair of mating green geckos, leering vacantly at her from the beamed ceiling directly overhead. As if struck by a cattle prod, C. King bolted for the shower, only to see an enormous *cucaracha* escaping down the drain. Feeling as though she had entered a nightmare, she threw on her clothes, grabbed her handbag and raced out the door. Perhaps a cup of strong, hot coffee and a brisk walk on the beach would help calm her nerves.

However, when she arrived at the beach, she found it less than hospitable. The storm had caused the ocean to vomit all its indigestible contents onto the sand. Tangled seaweed lay in heaps interspersed with a spew of bottles, cans and the general debris of an overindulgent and careless humanity. "Disgusting," she said to no one in particular, to humanity in general. Scowling, she made her way back up the cliff to the restaurant.

EARLY MORNING FOUND Inspector Neti Neti and Sergeant Shadow at the Ah So Retreat Center's Office confronting a half-awake Eduardo. They had relentlessly rung the bell until he at last appeared.

Neti Neti flashed his ID. "I need to see the registration information on your current guests right away."

Eduardo's jaw dropped. "Is there a problem? We've never had trouble here." He handed over the book and registration forms with a show of reluctance.

"We'll see about that," said Neti Neti as he eagerly pounced on the large black ledger.

He and Shadow spent some time jotting down the guest names and addresses. "How about the leader—Maya somebody?" he queried.

"She came a day early, so her information is on the

previous page," Eduardo explained rather pompously, trying to maintain an air of dignity, a difficult feat given his bathrobed and bleary-eyed condition.

They left him sitting behind the desk gazing at the tranquil scene beyond the lobby and wondering whether he ought to disturb the retreat center's senior management.

Back at the police station, Neti Neti lost no time e-mailing various U.S. law enforcement groups requesting background checks. "I'm uncovering something big here—*very* big." Neti Neti took a victorious sip from the cup of black coffee Shadow had brought him. "We should hear back soon. I put an 'Urgent' on all those requests," he told Shadow. "I need you down patrolling the Ah So Retreat Center's beach all day. Alert me immediately if you see anything unusual. That workshop is beyond a doubt the cover for a drug ring." He felt his adrenaline pump as he contemplated the impending arrests. "Go," he said sharply, trying to infuse the lumbering Shadow with some of his own sense of urgency.

THE SAND PATHS WERE ALREADY warm underfoot as the workshop members approached the meeting hall at nine A.M. The domed building was large and airy, and the double doors had been flung open invitingly. But a shared sense of dread gave the group reason to delay taking their seats inside.

Arturo Salinas, a small, stocky waiter and gardener at the retreat center, approached the group. After some hesitation, he singled out Betty and spoke in halting English. "Señora, er, Butter, er, Miss Maya asked me to give you this."

He handed Betty a note, which she worked to decipher. The handwriting was lavish with swirls and flourishes, all in a garish magenta ink. She read the note to the assembled group:

"Please serve the group this morning with anything they need, their cushions plumped, necks rubbed, water, etc. Remember, all good deeds enhance your chance for enlightenment."

As the group stared at her in disbelief, Betty grew her own shade of magenta from sheer humiliation. Everyone removed shoes and went inside to find their seats. Mona placed a comforting hand on her arm as she passed by. Still smarting, but inspired by the potential for good karma, Betty lingered, arranging the discarded shoes in two neat rows outside the door.

Maya entered, eyes flashing, veils swirling, and once again carrying with her a bewitching atmosphere.

Pere, always susceptible to mood, was certain he detected a strange shimmer surrounding Maya but immediately concluded it must be the new antihistamine he was taking.

Maya spoke, commanding immediate attention, "We have a lot of ground to cover today. This morning, there are several processes I wish to complete, and I want all of you to participate in each one. Even though it may not be *your* specific area needing improvement, I'm sure you will benefit. Then this afternoon, I will introduce you to my mini-courses designed to focus on your individual weaknesses. Now, if you will place your attention in the far right corner, you will observe the very latest purification tool. As you know, purification is essential for even the most rudimentary spiritual advancement. How can you possibly transcend into the more ethereal realms in your present state of heavy, earth-bound consciousness?"

They all turned to see Arturo plugging in an amazing black metal contraption with pulleys, a trapeze and flashing red lights.

My God, thought C. King, *it looks like a medieval torture device.* She had no sooner entertained this unsettling thought than Maya focused on her.

"Mrs. C. King," she said, "I would like you to be the first to experience the amazing powers of this New Age vibratory machine, the recently patented Purgaflush."

"I don't need this," C. King said. "I'm trying to live my life the right way." *Maybe some of the others who are not trying as hard as I, need this, the ones who cut corners, who get away with things I can't.*

Maya responded, "Then it is you who must demonstrate its astonishing powers. It will obviously have no effect on you but others here will follow your example and benefit. This is your chance to be a teacher."

C. King rose to the bait and allowed her bony, arthritic frame to be inserted into the machine. She experienced the terrifying sensation of being abruptly hoisted into the air where she hung suspended by her armpits. A bellows-like contraption covered her face and she heard the command, "Breathe deeply!" A strong vibration started at her feet and moved up her body. Her last realization before fainting was that she wasn't her body. Of course, she had read that, known that intellectually but this was different. Her body was hanging there, perhaps seriously injured, but who she was, was untouched, aware, watching.

It had all happened so fast that it caught the group off guard, and they stared in mute disbelief.

Then Sita, with unaccustomed intensity, inserted

herself between Maya and the machine and cried ferociously, "Get her out of there!"

Bossy and Govinda rushed over, and C. King was lowered to the floor, extracted from the contraption and revived, much to everyone's relief.

Maya, however, appeared unmoved by the shocked expressions around her. She directed Bossy and Govinda to help the weakened and unraveled C. King over to a cot in the corner where she promptly collapsed. She continued to shake but also marveled at her revelation. Betty hovered nearby to make sure she was all right.

Maya announced to the group, "Forget what you have just witnessed. This machine can efficiently remove the vibrations of lifetimes of bad karma. Arturo will assist those of you who wish purification, but before you line up, I would like to introduce you to two additional processes. You will have the remainder of the morning to explore them."

Pere, looking extremely pale, hissed, "She's not going to get me into that vicious contraption!"

Maya shot him a poisonous look and continued, "Spiritual seeking is the most elite identity that you can embrace here on earth. It places you above the masses who persist in mundane pursuits. You must perfect a spiritual identity that can be readily recognized and admired. There are certain postures, poses and attitudes that will set you apart. I am speaking about Mr. Govinda Go Go's particular request, I realize, but you can all gain from learning these strategies."

Ivanta whispered, "I certainly hope she won't disable anyone else."

Maya proceeded with instruction in 'above-it-all' attitudes, rigorous meditation postures, spiritual platitudes to sprinkle into conversations, and even dress codes that would set a spiritual seeker apart from the rest of humanity. She finished by saying, "Here is additional reading." She passed around thick pamphlets and then turned to Bossy.

"Mr. Baba Bossysatva, behind the curtain at the back of the room, is something that will greatly interest you and the rest of the group." Everyone turned with queasy foreboding. At this point, they had had enough experience with Maya to be extremely apprehensive as to what might be lurking behind the heavy black curtain.

Maya continued, "As you no doubt have heard, tantric practices enhance concentration and thus aid in the thrust toward enlightenment. The images you will experience behind the curtain will facilitate this. Now please proceed with your assignments, as there is much ground to cover and very little time." Then, casting a stern eye over the group, she departed.

AT NOON, THE LARGE DOORS to the retreat center's meeting hall burst open and like steam exploding from a pressure cooker, Bossy and Govinda led the escape. The others exited with only slightly more decorum. The high point of the day was to be a box lunch picnic at the beach, a two-hour diversion before the afternoon meeting commenced at two P.M. The group dispersed to gather bathing gear from their *palapas* and then rapidly reconvened at the beach below the retreat center's rocky cliff.

C. King was relieved to note the debris had been cleared from the sand.

Sita was maneuvering down the cliff in her recently purchased webbed sand sneakers. Her progress was unsteady and severely hampered by the webs, which kept snagging on the rocks. She was almost completely unrecognizable in an acid green bathing costume and tasseled, banana yellow sun hat, a recent flea market purchase.

Watching Sita as she made her final descent to the beach, Bossy had to suppress a fit of laughter; she resembled an ungainly toad wearing a lampshade. But Bossy's cruel assessment instantly turned to horror as he saw Sita slip and fall near the bottom of the incline.

She cried a plaintive, "Oh no!" as she landed face first in the sand. Bossy rushed to her aid and accidentally crushed her hat, while trying to avoid the fallout from her carpetbag, which had scattered over the sand.

Bossy exclaimed in a gentle inquiring voice, "My God, are you all right?"

"I guess I am," Sita said, brushing sand from her face. "It was stupid of me to wear these shoes! Thanks for your help."

"Anyone could have slipped here. The Center needs to build some steps down to the beach. They're the stupid ones!" Compassion welled up in Bossy as he looked in her eyes and saw her vulnerability. All his bravado vanished as he remembered a particularly painful event in his own life when he had taken a fall in a Physical Education class and everyone had laughed at him. He was touched by Sita's gratitude and he clearly saw, beyond the frumpy buffoonery of her comic appearance, directly into her good heart.

Several others had seen the accident and gathered around. They respectfully collected her belongings and offered words of support. Perhaps it was the morning's trauma with C. King that had unified them.

Sita was silent for once. Recognizing the genuine concern of the group, she was sobered to discover that they cared about her, just for herself. Bossy helped her get situated under a large beach umbrella near the others.

C. King was resting in the shade, mulling over the events of her difficult morning. She was grateful for the remarkable insight she'd gained about being more than simply her body. However, when thoughts about Maya Llusion surfaced again, she felt angry. She knew she should expose Maya to the authorities. *I'll attend the afternoon session, but only to gather more evidence of her dangerous methods.* She would speak with

Bossy about how and where to report Maya. The group would surely support her in this.

Betty and Mona wandered over to see how C. King was feeling and all three discussed how awful the morning had been. Betty said, "I've been to a lot of crazy, way-out workshops but this takes the cake."

Mona summed it up: "The woman's a dangerous fraud, and I think she must have some hidden agenda. Her attention doesn't seem to be on this workshop. It's pretty obvious she doesn't care about *us*. We should be very careful this afternoon and not let anyone get injured. I'm going to advise Sita not to allow those electrodes to be connected to her head."

"Right," Betty agreed. "One sure way to stop *thinking* is to permanently fry your brain."

Further down the beach, Bossy sat on a lounge chair next to Wu Wu. "Look down the beach to your right," Bossy said. "Isn't that one of the local guys we saw at the bar last night? He looks like a cop, doesn't he?"

"Yeah, and he seems to be watching us," Wu Wu replied. "I suppose they keep close tabs on all foreigners down here. After all, this part of the world is a haven for drug smugglers."

Sergeant Shadow and his highly trained drug dog, Snort, were indeed lurking a short distance down the beach. Bored with beach patrol, Shadow allowed himself to be pulled along by Snort, who appeared to be on the trail of something. The beagle was heading directly toward Bossy and Wu Wu.

The dog strained on his leash, dragging Sergeant Shadow along behind, and made a beeline for Wu Wu's open backpack, which had been tossed carelessly on the sand. In an instant, Snort began nosing voraciously through its contents. Wu Wu and Bossy sat up, amazed, while Shadow tried to prepare himself mentally for an arrest. He'd never actually caught a criminal before and his heart was racing.

"Hey, what's this?" Bossy jumped to his feet. "What the hell do you think you're doing?"

But before Shadow could reach for his gun or get a word out, Snort had extracted a brown paper bag from the pack and was tearing at it eagerly. He looked up, tail wagging; in his jaws, triumphantly displayed, was a chunk of something brown and leathery looking.

Bossy turned to Wu Wu, "*Beef jerky?* But I thought

you were a vegetarian! Ah well, don't we all have our little…." His voice trailed off.

Wu Wu hastened to cover his embarrassment. "I, er, I always carry a little something for stray dogs."

Meanwhile, Sergeant Shadow, clearly mortified, sensed he might be in the wrong line of work. He was still trying to come to peace with last night's entanglement with the shower curtain. Now, he had blundered into a perfectly innocent private beach party.

At that very moment, a panicked shriek came from the ocean, from Pere, who was flailing wildly about in deep water. The usually slow-moving Shadow dropped Snort's leash and ran to the water's edge, peeling off his clothes as he went. As Shadow dove into the ocean, his gigantic flamingo-printed boxer shorts ballooned out like a bright parasail.

Pere's screams of panic became demands as Shadow drew nearer. "Over here! Quick! I've been attacked! Hurry!"

Pere's cries roused the beach party, who all rushed to the water's edge. Ivanta arrived first and immediately began swimming out to rescue not only Pere, but Shadow as well. Shadow had reached Pere, only to be engulfed, as Pere wrapped his arms and legs around his savior like an octopus, pulling them both down. Realizing the seriousness of the situation, and with a few masterful strokes, Ivanta reached the desperately thrashing duo. With a neat karate chop, she released Pere's death grip and extracted the grateful Shadow. She grabbed Pere from behind and, with the confidence of a trained lifeguard, carried him back to shallow water. As she swam, she talked to him to help him relax. "You're safe now. I've got you. Let me do the work."

Shadow followed behind and arrived on the beach in time to hear Pere relating his ordeal. "I was just beginning to feel relaxed in the water. I could see clear to the bottom and I felt safe. All of a sudden this huge, ghostly thing with long tentacles appeared. Before I could get out of its way, it was, it was..."—he gave a head-to-toe shudder— "...all over me."

Pere lay down on a towel that Betty had brought over for him. Ivanta gently patted wet sand onto a fist-sized red welt on his leg.

"Ow," Pere winced, "it feels like a thousand porcupine quills sticking me!"

"You were probably stung by a Portuguese man-of-war jellyfish," Ivanta said. "I know quite a lot about them. I've read they're fairly common in these waters. The sand will help draw out the burning sensation. Just try to relax," she added kindly.

Mona offered her water bottle and Wu Wu, a homeopathic salve. "When I was in the Philippines, a jelly fish stung me," Wu Wu said. "It was excruciating!"

Pere looked at everyone, read their obvious concern and was deeply touched. His eyes met Ivanta's and he realized that, beneath the cool, aloof facade was a woman of great courage and compassion. Without a moment's hesitation, she'd put her own life in jeopardy to rescue him. Though it was often hard for him to speak about feelings, in this moment of gratitude, it came easily. He reached out and touched her arm. "I don't know what to say. You saved my life." He shook his head. "I've always let fear run my life. You, on the other hand, came fearlessly to my rescue."

Ivanta, who prided herself on detachment, was nevertheless moved by Pere's words and by her own sense of openness and caring. "Anyone would have done as much," she said, lowering her eyes.

Pere then turned to Shadow. "I don't even know you, but I owe you a debt of gratitude for ignoring your own safety trying to save me. I'm sorry that I almost drowned us both. I was just so frightened." Snort came over to Pere and licked him, leaving a sandy lather on Pere's leg.

Awash with relief, Pere realized, *I almost died out there. I could so easily have died. The end can come at any time, for any of us.*

The crowd gradually dispersed, assured that Pere was all right. Betty and Govinda dashed into shallow water and began splashing each other in obvious delight.

Eduardo was picking his way down the steep path to the beach, balancing a mountain of box lunches, when he overheard Mona exclaim, "Oh good, here comes food. I'm starved."

Just then another scream pierced the air, and once again everyone turned. This time it was Betty who, in a playful lunge at Govinda, had popped out of the top of her scanty bikini. Eduardo lurched precariously forward, attempting to steady his teetering load as he beheld this deliciously startling sight. Riveted, he watched as Betty frantically tried to cover her breasts with one hand while scrambling after the errant wisp of bathing suit. The top floated over to Govinda, who grabbed it, unhesitatingly returned it to Betty, and then gallantly turned his back to shield her from view. After collecting herself into her swimsuit, Betty emerged from behind Govinda wearing a modest Mona Lisa smile.

Eduardo, who had come perilously close to turning the seaside picnic into a seagull smorgasbord, regained his composure. Assuming a look of bored indifference, he distributed the lunches and retreated back up the hillside.

After eating, most of the group reluctantly returned to their rooms. Only C. King, Bossy and Sita lingered in the warmth of the early afternoon sun. Mona, having decided there was time for a quick dip before the next session, was floating in the calm water just beyond the surf, apparently unconcerned about Portuguese man-of-war jellyfish. She had arrived at the beach prepared to be the center of attention because she was modeling a unique, shimmering bathing suit made of Japanese organic rice paper. But she had been upstaged by Sita's fall and Pere's near-drowning. Now, aware that the noon break was ending, she emerged from the water to find her desire for attention immediately fulfilled—all eyes were upon her. Looking down, she gasped, for where her suit had once been there was only a glistening, wasabi green imprint on her body. C. King rushed toward Mona with a large beach towel as Mona exclaimed ruefully, "How was I to know that my suit would dissolve in salt water? The label was in Japanese!"

Bossy made no attempt to hide his appreciation of the moment and let out an unbridled guffaw, while Sita realized, not for the first time that day, that she wasn't the only one who'd had occasion to feel foolish.

THE SUN HAD DIPPED BEHIND the palms as the nine participants gathered at the bar. They'd spent the afternoon exploring the mini-courses Maya Llusion had assigned. As the day progressed, Maya had seemed increasingly distracted and had offered precious little help or encouragement. By day's end, all felt that the workshop had been shallow bordering on the absurd. Everyone was relieved when the farce finally ended. To help submerge a general feeling of gloom, and perhaps other more volatile emotions, they'd gathered around an array of vivid tropical drinks. Bossy pulled a few tables together and they all drew up chairs. Talk erupted.

"Unbelievable," C. King burst out, unable to restrain herself another moment. "I can't imagine Maya thought she could get away with peddling such useless, preposterous spiritual pap. I should have heeded my own instincts and skipped today's meeting. The woman *must* be exposed, endangering us with that life-threatening purification contraption. At my age, I could have had a heart attack and died. And that helmet thing bristling with electrodes that she tried to force onto your head, Sita! Thank God, you refused!"

C. King's indignation triggered Bossy's own outrage. "It was a total waste." Bossy had lost control more than once during the day, and had ended up shouting in Maya Llusion's face. Finally, Maya had simply ignored him. "That Tantric Tension Enhancing Ritual is nothing more than a plagiarized version of one I developed for one of my own workshops. I should sue her!"

"Well," Betty said, "that tantric stuff was kind of interesting," adding quickly, "but nothing I didn't already know."

"Maya teaches by intimidation and that doesn't work for me," Ivanta said. "And I know more in my little finger about *cenotes* than she'll ever know!"

Govinda joined the furor. "The way she pressured us into enduring all those stupid processes was insulting. She treated us like spiritual novices. I suppose she thinks she can get away with things like that, but I've been around the block a few times and it doesn't cut it with me. When I cornered her about Expando, she wasn't even slightly interested. This has been a total waste of my time. I can't imagine there's one of us who feels any further along the spiritual path."

"That's certainly true," agreed Ivanta.

Even Sita was visibly upset. "I could have ended up like you, C. King, unconscious or even electrocuted. I really don't know what prompts me to attend these things."

Mona said, "Aren't you, deep down, just like the rest of us, hoping for a spiritual awakening?"

"Not enough to endure any more ridiculous workshops," Sita replied. She sighed deeply, folded her arms across her chest and retreated back into lethargy.

Mona turned to Pere. "How's your leg, by the way?"

"Not too bad. Wu Wu's salve helps. But my nervous system can't tolerate any more of this craziness. I was right to be suspicious of Maya. She's a tyrant! I came here to find peace and safety, yet I've never felt less safe."

"I'm mad enough to kill!" Bossy exclaimed. "Maya's misrepresentation of the spiritual path must be stopped. It taints the rest of us teachers."

"I support you," Wu Wu said, having fallen from cloud nine with a painful thud. "She gave me that impossible past life task and offered no concrete suggestions for implementing it, which only adds to my frustration. It's certainly a far cry from any state of bliss! You're dead right, Bossy, something has to be done."

"Please don't do anything violent," Betty pleaded.

"Right," Sita remarked. "After all, nothing's really lost but a few days. Perhaps we can turn this into a pleasant tropical vacation. I always say, 'When you have lemons, make lemonade.' I can remember many times in my life when I've done just that. There was that event in Fresno when the guru didn't ..."

"What happened to your anger?" Mona interrupted. "I'd still be angry if I were you. Maya's insinuation that you're unconscious was so hurtful! I was very upset when she told you that."

Sita yawned and sucked on her drink. "I just let those things roll off me. You know, 'Don't sweat the small stuff.'"

Aggravated by Sita's complacence, Bossy bellowed, "I'm going to do her in. She's a fraud and she simply hasn't delivered the goods!" His voice echoed through the bar.

"I'M GOING TO DO HER IN. She's a fraud and she hasn't delivered the goods!" were the first words Inspector Neti Neti and his sergeant heard as they entered the bar. The inspector was already basking in the glory of a most satisfying day, and this overheard comment iced his cake. E-mail replies had been coming in all day and with some very curious information. Neti Neti's suspicions about the workshop leader had been justified. Maya Llusion had more than once been accused of misrepresentation, false advertising and mental harassment.

The reports on the others had turned up a few minor offenses and suspicious occurrences. He pulled out his list. He wanted to match the names on his list with the faces in the bar, pairing possible crimes with the perpetrators. He beckoned to Eduardo, who was assisting at the bar that evening.

"Which is Pere Anoiananda?" he demanded.

"The one in the Hawaiian shirt," Eduardo said, remembering how badly the group had treated him as they'd checked in.

"Ah ha," Neti Neti said under his breath. He nudged Shadow, pointing an accusing finger at Pere's name on the list. "Look at this: 'Cited for abuse of the 9-1-1 emergency number.' One month he called three times, all false alarms."

He turned to Eduardo. "And which one is Mona Preen?"

Enjoying his role as deputy crime-solver, Eduardo pointed to Mona. "She's the one who arrived with a dozen suitcases."

Neti Neti couldn't hide his delight. "Shoplifting. Only 'suspicion of,' but enough for our purposes." He consulted his list. "What about Baba Bossysatva?" Then he snorted, "What weird names these people have. Probably made them up when they were high on drugs!"

"Bossysatva is that big man in the blue shirt,"

Eduardo told him.

Shadow peered at the list. "He's the one who had a part time job as a bouncer at a bar. Says here, he brained a guy with a bottle of thirty-year-old, single-malt scotch. Seems the nightclub owner thought he should have used a bottle of beer. The customer recovered, but our man was still charged."

"What about this one?" Neti Neti persisted, pointing to a name on the list, "Miss Betty Butterup."

"Oh, she's the cute one with the sexy come-on," Eduardo replied.

"Figures," said the inspector. "She was cited last summer in Sheboygan, Wisconsin for stalking."

Neti Neti moved his index finger down to the next name on the list, Mrs. Sita Sofa. He looked at Eduardo, who nodded toward Sita. The inspector smiled and read aloud: "'Reckless backing.' Seems she spent one night in jail while under investigation for backing into a cop on a motorcycle. Bet *that* ticket set her back a few pesos."

Eduardo glanced at the next name on the list. "Miss Ivanta B. Alone is sitting next to Mrs. Sofa."

"She's clean," Shadow announced.

"I doubt it," said Neti Neti dismissively. "She's just covered her tracks well."

"And Mrs. C. King?" asked Shadow. Eduardo pointed at C. King, who was sitting in an aura of sanctity, sipping her drink.

Neti Neti sniffed, disappointed. "Nothing on her, but she no doubt has a secret life. That kind often does. Which one is Govinda Go Go? He's been involved in numerous pyramid schemes."

"Govinda's the handsome one who is always talking on his cell phone," said Eduardo.

"Okay, just one more. Someone named—can you can believe it?—Wu Wu Way."

"That's easy," laughed Eduardo. "He is the one who looks like he has helium balloons tied to his wrist and is floating about a foot off the ground. Pretty flaky, I'd say."

Wu Wu's background information was the closest Neti Neti had found to a drug link. "He was the proprietor of a head shop in Los Angeles where they sold waterbeds, water pipes, bongs, and other drug paraphernalia."

It was so gratifying to have his hunches confirmed.

Ecstatic, Neti Neti said to Eduardo, "Get me a double pineapple Marguerita."

AT THE BAR, MONA LOOKED around at the discontented group. They'd all started to seem like friends to her. "I know we're disappointed—no one more than I. We've come here for enlightenment, and it's pretty clear we all have an idea of what enlightenment should be like." She turned to Govinda who was seated next to her, "I'm really interested to know—did you come here believing enlightenment would help you become more effective in the business world?"

"That would be splendid, of course," Govinda said, "but I'm beginning to see that *real* happiness might come from more than that. I've discovered that I've made work my entire life and identity, and I have no idea who I am without it. Even spiritual seeking has been like a career for me. But last night, when the electricity failed, I actually panicked. All my available distractions were suddenly gone. I felt empty and had to admit the idea of having nothing to do is quite terrifying to me. I imagine, if I were enlightened, I'd be comfortable with the experience of having nothing to do."

The group was somewhat taken aback by Govinda's honesty. It opened the door for others.

Ivanta said, "I've imagined that self-realization would protect me from constant intrusions into my privacy."

C. King said, "I've always hoped that enlightenment would help me rise above the chaotic human condition. Now I wonder if maybe it'll bring the realization that everything's perfect just as it is, chaos and all."

"I really don't have any idea how I got involved with this whole searching thing," Sita said. "It just kind of happened, and now I wish I'd never started."

"Well, I'm glad that I did," Wu Wu said, "I figure enlightenment will lift me, permanently above my *ordinary* self—I'm counting on it! I'm not good at wallowing about in the boring, day-to-day human condition."

"I've always thought that if I ever got enlightened,

I'd be able to accept myself the way I am," Betty said. "Now it feels quite hopeless. Maya made it clear enlightenment for me will only occur, if it *ever* occurs, sometime off in the distant future."

"Nah, don't get discouraged," Bossy said, "I'm sure we can all become enlightened. But it's going to take a lot of dedication and the right approach. And, as I've said before, Maya's way is the wrong way."

"You're right, Bossy," Pere said. "Maya's Seven Principles are impossible. I had an insight today when I almost drowned. I realized how much attention I've given to trying to stay safe. I've been hoping enlightenment would help me feel safe and protected. But today it was the *unsafe* that opened my heart."

Mona said, "That's wonderful, Pere! I certainly need more than just some shallow version of recognition and love. I want to live authentically and I need to find out what that really means. Right now, it's just a spiritual catch phrase. Maya Llusion's good at throwing those around. But you know, maybe it's not up to Maya or any teacher, in fact, to lead us to enlightenment. Maybe it's an inside job. And even if Maya's a charlatan, don't you all feel there's something mysterious and intense about this place that's pushing us toward what we *really* want?"

There was silence as they felt the truth of her words. Why *had* they come to Tulum? What did they *really* want?

In a reflective mood, they rose and went in to dinner.

After they were seated once again at the round table and had ordered their meals, C. King said, "Maybe this experience with Maya Llusion is forcing us to take a look at spiritual seeking. Does it really *get* us anywhere? If we hadn't been put into this impossible situation, we might have gone on jumping through hoops, believing if we searched hard enough or found just the right teacher or method, that would bring us enlightenment. I have to admit that after years of seeking, I'm no closer to enlightenment."

There was general agreement followed by an uncomfortable silence as they all pondered their individual feelings of internal disarray.

Struck by the serious turn the conversation had taken, Wu Wu said, "You realize, we don't have to stay here. Let's call the shuttles and go to Cancun. We could be dancing to *mariachi* music instead of sitting here feeling let down." But even as he heard himself, an inner knowing came to him. He recognized that familiar pattern of escaping into the next experience. This time it wouldn't work.

Sita said, "I really don't know why we have to create this feeling of conflict with what has happened. The workshop's a bust, but that's no reason to lose our cool. Can't we find some way to stay centered? Maybe this entire experience is God's will. Maybe there are no accidents. Of course, I *want* peace, serenity. I just keep telling myself, one day my ship will come in." With this homey aphorism she settled back comfortably in her chair.

"I couldn't disagree more," Bossy said to Sita. "I don't think it's God's will that we submit placidly to a rip-off."

"I certainly agree, Bossy," C. King said. "There's no reason to attend tomorrow's session, but I do want to confront Maya. I'd really like to get my money back."

Everyone thought this was a good idea and agreed to unite in challenging Maya. They lingered at the table, watching the candles burn low and feeling their newly forged companionship. No one was eager to rush off to the solitude of a *palapa*.

Evening found Maya attempting to relax on the patio of her *palapa*, waiting for the cover of darkness. It had been a stressful day, an awful day, really. The workshop participants were clearly disenchanted with her program. And she knew she'd been only half-attentive to their individual needs. But she had far more serious matters on her mind. She'd come here with the intention of gaining access to one of the special vortices of power, a *cenote* in the nearby Tulum ruins. In this cavern there was believed to be a dynamic convergence of transformative energies.

She'd recently procured copies of some ancient occult texts on the art of amassing and controlling these energies. The long-lost codices had been unearthed by archaeologists working at the Tulum ruins, and by dubious means, Maya had acquired partial translations and spent her spare time pouring over the confusing, esoteric text for clues. She had confirmed that a powerful secret chamber was located nearby, but she wasn't sure of its exact location. She had approached several of the retreat center workers, attempting to bribe them into showing her the site, but no one could help her. The sacred *cenote* was said to be guarded by spells, rendering it invisible and inaccessible to all but those with the power to discern its portal. Maya wanted to believe she had this power, but, after hours of searching, she'd failed to find the holy place.

By now, she was almost desperate. The workshop would soon end and she was due to leave for London.

She stared at the confusing text, willing it to yield answers, but nothing came to her. Frustrated, she crushed the unfathomable manuscript in her hands.

But wait! Maybe she could use the document itself as a kind of dowsing tool to guide her to the *cenote!*

Brilliant, she thought, smoothing out the crushed manuscript. She rolled it into a tight cylindrical wand, a divining rod. Invigorated by this inspired approach, she waved her 'wand' about and imagined it invested with sufficient power and intention to lead her to her destination.

She'd spent each night wandering the cliffs, searching among the ruins and rock formations for the elusive chamber. Tonight, shrouded in her darkest veils and pleased at her creativity, she slipped silently into the night, magic scepter in hand.

She made her way to the ruins and, once there, allowed herself to follow the bidding of the wand as it guided her along the edge of the cliff and through the ruins with its maze of giant stones. All at once, she felt herself drawn into a dark passage through an opening in the rocks.

This must be it! The cenote! Excitedly, she groped her way down into the impenetrable darkness. One hand clutching the document and the other feeling her way through the narrow passageway, she inched down the steep, uneven ground. As she continued forward, messianic fantasies played out in her mind amid the gloom: She would become a different person, one with unimaginable power. She would bring an entirely new approach to her teaching, amazing embellishments.

Her following would increase. Her fame would be world-wide.

Fueled by these fantasies, Maya continued to inch forward and felt an atmosphere of immense power surrounding her that made her feel suddenly weak and dizzy. She reached her hand out to her left and met only space. Cautiously, she crept along until she encountered a cold stone wall. She leaned against it for balance and breathed a sound which echoed around the cavern walls. She was definitely in a large place. The blackness was impervious, except for faint gleams of light that appeared to be coming from two small apertures overhead. She leaned her back against the wall and carefully arranged herself in a receptive posture to await instruction.

Maya slowly became aware of a profound silence. She felt an intense, vibrantly alive presence permeating her entire being and, as before, the terror of being overtaken seized her. Shuddering violently, she slumped to the earthen floor as a great fear of losing herself enveloped her.

"You can't frighten me! I am *not* a part of You! *I* am more powerful than *You!*"

She knew she must not give in.

She cried out again, "I will *never* submit to You!"

Maya felt faint and crazed. The walls of the *cenote* seemed to close in on her. She felt she would be crushed. She was sucked into the swirling black hole of her own profound resistance and terror.

IN THE DINING ROOM, QUANTOMUNDI observed the group and waited for an opportunity to approach. The candles on the round table finally burned low. Quantomundi watched as the clearly disheartened companions pushed back their chairs and slowly made their way out the door, into the night. Quantomundi quietly followed.

■ □ ■

Neti Neti had noticed Quantomundi in the dining room, and now watched from his table with great interest. Shadow sat with him, finishing his meal.

This particular shaman had been a festering thorn in Neti Neti's side since his assignment to Tulum.

Partly it was the shaman's widespread influence. But also, Neti Neti understood that the old shamanistic rituals involved the use of hallucinogens. In Mexico, a shaman's immunity under the law was tacitly recognized and honored, but any use of drugs rankled the inspector's sense of right and wrong. (What Neti Neti did not know was that Quantomundi's wisdom was not—*had never been*—inspired by drugs of any kind.)

Fueled by the various incriminating conversations he'd overheard and the bizarre behavior of the workshop participants, and now the presence of this shaman who was following the group, Neti Neti's fertile mind put two and two together: It all spelled *drugs*. Mobilized, Neti Neti leapt up from the table to trail Quantomundi. Shadow put down his fork and reluctantly followed. As the two stood in the shadows of the building, they saw the shaman advance toward the seekers.

THE NIGHT WAS ENCHANTING. The group paused, momentarily relieved of their distress by the sight of the silver sea reflecting the light of the full moon.

The shaman approached them. In perfect and only slightly accented English he said, "Please forgive me for intruding on your group. My name is Quantomundi. I'm a local shaman. I've watched you the last two nights and couldn't help but notice your confusion and disillusionment."

Everyone turned to him, surprised and curious.

He said simply, "It *is* possible to experience clarity."

Bossysatva, in his role as protector, stepped forward. "We don't need help! For the past two days, we've been subjected to a masterful display of hocus-pocus and spiritual double-talk."

Unmoved, Quantomundi exuded compassion for Bossy's distress. Everyone stared at the shaman, his noble posture and unmistakable aura of integrity made even more dramatic by the moonlight.

"I can understand your suspicion, but if you listen to what I have to say, you may realize that you are hearing what you have always known but overlooked."

Just then, Pere surprised everyone by abruptly moving forward. Despite his inner trembling, he spoke with strength and directness. "I'm fed up with being afraid. Fear has tormented me all my life. I'm tired of being confused. I, for one, will not let my doubts prevent me from hearing what this man has to say."

Pere's resolute statement rang true. A sudden gust of wind charged the still night. It seemed like an omen. There was power in the moment and everyone felt it.

Quantomundi said, "Come with me."

Silently they followed to a nearby clearing where they settled on stone benches in the moonlight to hear what Quantomundi had to say. Their receptivity was reflected in the complete attention each person now gave to the shaman.

He spoke with quiet authority. "What I am about to say may sound strange or even radical but I sense that there is a real yearning for clarity in this group. I also sought answers about life, and this is what was revealed: When we are very young and innocent, there is no recognition of ourselves as individuals, no sense of an 'I' who is separate from everything and everyone else. We are simply pure being, unable to differentiate between ourselves and others.

"Then the game of hide-and-seek begins. We are taught the doctrine of separation. The 'I' thought emerges, and the moment it does, there is a sense of loss, often unconscious. We may feel we have lost our inner home, our sense of safety and our natural knowing that we *are* unconditional love. Some of you might recall the actual moment of self-recognition, when you began to relate to the world through your body, your mind and your personality. At that moment, you began to believe in the illusion of separation.

"However, things aren't always as they seem. Everyone and everything is eternal light and out of this light manifests an amazing divine drama. If William

Shakespeare had been the playwright, he might have called it 'The Light Seeking the Light.' All the actors in the drama have their own unique script and most completely identify with their roles. All are seeking in their own way. In the scenes played on the 'Stage of Life,' actors are looking for satisfaction and completion through power, relationships, sex, religion, and everything else that could ever be imagined. The drama is fascinating because it contains all of creation in its endless possibility.

"Some of the players have parts that allow them to have a faint memory of the joy of Oneness, and these players seek to regain it. Other characters do not consciously remember at all. Some have scripts in which there is an awakening to the truth—that separation from Oneness is an illusion.

"Here is the important point: It doesn't matter what part is played because whatever happens in the divine drama cannot, in the least, affect the light of awareness that is playing all the parts. And without that light, there would be: no theater, no drama, no actors."

"Why doesn't it matter?" someone asked. "The role I'm playing matters a lot, at least to me."

"What is your name?" asked Quantomundi.

"Govinda."

Quantomundi explained, "There is no individual playing a role. *You,* as the light of awareness, are playing the role of 'Govinda.' "

Govinda said emphatically, "But I'm *here.* I'm *alive.* I can *feel* myself."

Quantomundi said, "This feeling of aliveness or presence is who you are. The apparent individual, called 'Govinda,' is only a thought or idea in consciousness. The illusion of a separate self is very powerful, but there *isn't* one. Look inside. You will not be able to find an individual. There is a sense of aliveness, the awareness of body sensations, thoughts and feelings; but can you find a solid, concrete *you?*"

Quantomundi paused while Govinda closed his eyes and searched. Finally, Govinda said, "I can't actually find a person, but there is awareness, an absolute knowing of everything that is happening right now. It feels very familiar."

"That's right!" said Quantomundi. "It feels familiar because awareness is your true nature. Oneness is playing a game, pretending to lose itself in its own creation. The game is called 'the divine drama,' a masterful theatrical illusion that appears to be real but it is all make-believe. When you leave the theater after seeing a play, you know that when the curtain comes down, the actors cease being actors. They take off their costumes and know that nothing *real* actually happened. It's just like that."

"Then what's the purpose of the divine drama?" asked Ivanta.

Quantomundi answered, "There is no purpose. I suppose you could say that unconditional love delights in all its endless forms. It is a mystery and a miracle."

"Yes, I see," said Ivanta softly. "Sometimes I feel tremendous gratitude simply for the privilege of being alive."

Betty spoke, the quivering in her voice revealing despair, "Why do I feel that I have to get rid of the parts of my character that I don't like, in order to live in Oneness?"

Quantomundi answered reassuringly, "I'm talking about an absolute shift in perception. If you are aware that you are Oneness playing a part in a cosmic drama, there is no need to get rid of or change anything to know what you really are." Then he added with emphasis, "No amount of mental understanding will reveal this, but this truth can be heard and, in an instant, a shift to clarity can occur."

Bossy spoke up, "But *who* makes the shift? Isn't the search for enlightenment all about the seeker, who, through intense seeking, finally wakes up from the dream?"

"That is a *very* common misconception." replied Quantomundi. "When awakening happens, what is seen is that there has always been present awareness, and there is nothing but Oneness. There is no individual seeker who could ever wake up."

"That's a bombshell for the mind!" said Bossy as he thought back on all his years of esoteric practices.

"Yes, it is. The mind doesn't know what to do with this," admitted Quantomundi. He continued speaking from deep inner conviction. "Who you are cannot be defined by anything that happens in the dream. However, each moment of the dream-drama invites the possibility of being awake in the dream as a lucid dreamer. You are pure awareness in which the dream of manifestation appears. It all appears *in* you. You are the light which lights up the world stage. Each moment, the content of awareness is a perfect divine expression, just as it is."

Now, visibly upset, Bossy interrupted. "You call this enlightened? A perfect divine expression? You should meet our workshop leader. You live here in this remote paradise. What about the rest of the world?"

"Right," Wu Wu added, "What about suffering? Suffering doesn't fit into the definition of enlightenment. Enlightenment promises constant bliss."

"Ah, but *everything* you see is an expression of Oneness, including bliss, suffering, *and* your workshop leader."

C. King whispered, "A perfect divine expression, just as I am. That would change everything."

After a reflective silence, Mona said, "Sometimes I feel that I'm acting in a play but I'm afraid I'd be lost without a role. Now, as I listen to you, I can recall moments of silence, of peace, when I have been without my props, my script and costumes."

"Yes," replied Quantomundi, "And that silence is your true nature. It can never be lost."

"When I feel fear, it seems real," Pere declared. "I

can feel it in my body. It takes me over."

Quantomundi asked, "What is noticing this? What sees everything?" He paused, then continued, "Fear can appear—does appear—in the drama as part of the script. There is *no one* that is experiencing fear. One-ness *as fear* is appearing in the moment. With awakening comes the realization that any part in the drama can be played without becoming lost in that part."

Pere mused out loud, "I always thought the fear was real and I needed to find a refuge from it."

"Only the mind seeks a refuge. Who you are does not need refuge," the shaman replied.

"I wish I really knew that," said Pere.

"You do!"

Wu Wu felt he needed to ask, "Don't you believe that examining lessons from our past lives can help?"

Quantomundi smiled tenderly at him. "One illusory life story is enough."

Sita asked, "My mind is very active. Don't I need to stop all that thinking?"

"Impossible!" Quantomundi said. "Who is going to do that? The mind is also Oneness. Thoughts appear and disappear like clouds in the sky. Thoughts do not define who you are."

"That's a relief," sighed Sita.

C. King spoke up: "I've worked very hard for many years to be enlightened, but seeking has gotten me nowhere. Why haven't I awakened?"

Quantomundi answered, "Enlightenment can never occur for a personal self, because there isn't one. Awareness is eternally awake to everything, but a dreamed character can never awaken. What *you* are is always present, no matter what is apparently happening. Feel the aliveness and rest in the immediate, tangible sense of being which always is."

Silence fell upon the group and each one felt as though their mind had been stunned. They had never, in all their years of seeking, heard such a radical message—yet they instinctively felt, deep within, the truth that had been spoken.

Quantomundi too, was silent for a while. Then he continued, "I know of a very special place where we can all sit together. Years ago, it helped me absorb the truth. It is a sacred cave called a *cenote*. It is well hidden but very near."

Ivanta was unable to contain herself. "This is the

cavern I have been reading about! But it is very sacred. Are we ready to enter such a holy place?"

Quantomundi spoke, "This is not about being worthy or unworthy. Leave your beliefs about yourselves behind and come with me to the *cenote*." They followed him out of the clearing and toward the cliff.

■ □ ■

Neti Neti and Shadow had been crouching in the shrubbery that surrounded the clearing. Because of his bulk, Shadow had difficulty kneeling. Every now and then his haunches emitted a loud creak and he groaned with pain.

Unable to get close enough to hear every word of the conversation, they still caught enough for the inspector to confirm his suspicions involving the *cenote* caves, altered states of consciousness, and drugs. Even in this moment of triumph, he dared not move too quickly. As he helped untangle Shadow from the foliage, it occurred to him that surveillance with Shadow was rather like tracking prey with an elephant for a companion.

Fearing they'd be spotted in the bright moonlight, they followed at a discreet distance.

QUANTOMUNDI AND THE GROUP had almost reached the area where the *cenote* was hidden, when a scream pierced the night. Startled, they turned toward the sound in time to see Maya Llusion emerge from the ruins. She streaked along the cliff edge, veils billowing out like sails in a high wind. She ran as if crazed and, in the dramatic spotlight of the moon, her form cast eerie shadows. They watched spellbound as Maya made an abrupt turn and appeared to trip on her veils.

Then, before their eyes, she plunged over the cliff's edge.

Everyone raced to the edge of the precipice, to the spot from which Maya had vanished. They peered over and saw only the surf crashing on the rocks below.

"Oh my God!" exclaimed Bossy. The others gasped in horror. Then a stunned silence fell over the group.

In that moment, each of the nine simultaneously felt a profound shift in consciousness, as if a hypnotic trance, which had prevented the direct experience of being, had suddenly lifted.

Neti Neti and Shadow, trailing at a distance, also heard the scream and saw Maya Llusion tumble over the cliff's edge. Inexplicably, they too experienced the same opening into being.

They ran to the precipice, joining Quantomundi and the others, to scan the sea below for any sign of Maya Llusion. But the vast ocean of consciousness had swallowed her whole. It had happened so quickly that the searchers wondered if they had imagined it. They looked at each other with the dawning realization of what part Maya Llusion played in the divine drama. The exquisite cosmic game of pretending to be separate from Oneness was revealed

"Well I'll be damned. I realize I've always known this," Bossy exclaimed, joining Shadow in mutual amazement.

Released from the thrall of the stories woven by his mind, Pere ran wildly through the group shouting, "Hallelujah!"

Neti Neti's self-deception fell away. Grinning from ear to ear, he grabbed Betty and spun her round and round, both lost in the bliss of existence.

Mona fell into the truest sense of herself beyond all definitions.

Ivanta was enfolded in all-inclusive openness.

For all, there was an energetic shift from contracted separation to wholeness.

C. King turned to Quantomundi in awe. "There's nothing left but gratitude."

Wu Wu added, "And the celebration of each moment."

"Yes," Quantomundi replied.

In his wisdom, Quantomundi knew that seeing life as a lucid dream did not mean necessarily ignoring the dream. Maya Llusion's disappearance must be reported. Not wanting to disturb the ecstatic police officer's direct sense of liberation, he slipped away to the retreat center's Office. On the way, he encountered Eduardo, who had overheard the joyful commotion and had come out to see what all the ruckus was about.

"What's going on?" the clerk demanded. He looked

across the way at the group on the cliff. They appeared to be dancing in the moonlight. He chuckled. "Guess they've had a few too many drinks."

"Mm," replied Quantomundi. "I need to make a phone call."

"Certainly," said Eduardo. Then curiosity got the better of him. "Why? I mean, it's awfully late."

Quantomundi followed him to the Office and phoned the Tulum police station. There was no answer. He left a message describing the accident on the cliff's edge and how several witnesses had been powerless to prevent it. He then left a rather stunned Eduardo to rejoin the group.

Once more gathering together, they looked at each other—the shaman, the group of nine, and the two policemen—and saw only Oneness in all its forms. The divine drama was exposed. It was clear that the play would go on. The actors and stories would continue to appear and disappear, but the light of awareness which illuminates the Theater of Life would remain ever-constant.

ACT III

Despite the fact that it was Sunday morning, Neti Neti found himself seated at his familiar desk at the police station. Late in the night, Quantomundi told him that he had informed the Tulum police about Maya Llusion's plunge over the cliff. Neti Neti supposed he *should* call his boss to give him his rendition of last night's accident, but somehow it didn't seem all that important. An inner silence had enveloped him and now, in that profound stillness, the phone jangled.

At the other end, Chief Superintendent Ramon Stompedo's deep voice rumbled, "Where in the hell have you been? Don't you realize that there has been a disappearance—possibly a murder—at that weird retreat center, right under your nose!" The growling voice ranted on about a missing body and witnesses.

Neti Neti placed the receiver quietly on the desk and, without a backward glance, he walked out the door and made his way to the beach. He removed his shoes, his jacket and all the trappings that supported his identity. He felt like he had been living in a dream, a dream where everything that had mattered a great deal, now, suddenly, did not. What mattered was this intense feeling of aliveness, the soft sand beneath his bare feet, the early morning sun warm on his back.

A large figure approached him. It was his sergeant and the dog, Snort, no longer on a leash but bounding in circles and frolicking in the sand.

Shadow shaded his eyes from the sun and looked at Neti Neti. "Quite a night, wasn't it?" he said with a slight smile. "Did that woman really fall off the cliff or did we imagine it? I mean, there was nobody near her and no one's found her body, have they? Moonlight can play tricks with the eyes, you know." They ambled along companionably. Then Shadow said, "I realized last night, something I figure I've known for some time, that I'm really not cut out for detective work. It was always hard for me to take sides. I could see everyone's point of view. And now, after last night, I know that being a policeman isn't the role I want to play. I'm going to quit the force, find Snort here a nice lady friend, and raise and sell little Snorts. That's really all I'm drawn to." He bent down to affectionately pat the beagle's sandy back.

Neti Neti nodded in understanding. He too had experienced a shift in perception and was rapidly rearranging his priorities. He said to Shadow, "The chief was on the phone this morning insisting that I get right on the case. Both you and I know it was an accident, the body was probably washed out to sea, and my report will say just that."

Shadow was shocked at Neti Neti's loss of ambition. Gone were the zeal and ardor that Shadow had tried in vain to emulate. The boss he had known had been so intense, but now here was this relaxed and barefoot person. "Well, I have to get going," he said. "I'll call the Chief and let him know I've quit."

"Good luck, Salvadore," said Neti Neti shaking his hand.

"Thanks, sir," replied Shadow. "I hope to see you around."

Neti Neti turned toward the sea and became lost in his surroundings. He had no idea how long he had been standing there when he heard someone call his name. He turned to see Betty tripping across the beach. The queer sensation in his stomach was very much the same as he'd experienced the night before while dancing with Betty on the cliff.

She looked delighted to see him. "You're out early."

He nodded, equally pleased to see her. Then, looking down, he mumbled, "Thought you'd be with the others this morning, making plans to leave."

Betty grinned and moved closer to him. "I've changed my plans. I've no desire to go back to Sheboygan, not after last night. I like it here. It's perfect. I just might open a little taco stand on the beach. Care to flip a few tortillas with me?" They looked at each other and laughed.

■ □ ■

Back at the retreat center, the rest of the group had gathered in the dining hall for breakfast.

As C. King sat down, Bossy remarked, "You know,

Charlotte, I do believe you look twenty years younger."

She toyed with the sedate collar of pearls around her neck, which did not go in the least with the brilliant, wildly patterned sarong she'd borrowed from Mona. In a giddy voice, she said, "What was all the seriousness about? Who is there to be responsible? The weight of the world has been lifted."

Bossy replied, "You're right! I can't stop laughing! I've been laughing all night. Pere and I sat up for hours howling with relief. I suppose we should have been somber, given the circumstances, Maya falling over the cliff. But the whole thing seems unreal to me, like a movie."

Mona nodded in agreement. "It did seem like a stage set last night, didn't it? The cliff, back-lit by moonlight and that dark figure weaving around on the precipice and then suddenly disappearing. I know we all wanted to be free of her, but not *that* way. Truth is, Maya wasn't the only illusion to disappear last night; what I had thought of as *me* is gone too. Life goes on, scene after scene, yet there isn't an individual *me* it's happening to. There's no longer a self-obsessed *star* appearing in her own personal soap opera."

Govinda cleared his throat and smiled mischievously. "How extraordinary to discover that what I most feared—*emptiness*—is what I *am*."

"That's a huge realization, Govinda," Pere said. "You know, it all comes down to a simple case of mistaken identity."

"It's almost impossible to talk about," Sita said. "Wu Wu and I had early coffee and tried to put all this into words but I ended up tongue-tied. Quite a switch for a nonstop talker!"

"Ah," Ivanta sighed, "There's enormous relief. It's so *simple*—so ordinary—yet such a wonder. *This is it.*" Then she added with a sweeping gesture, "All there is, is this."

Bossy said with a smile, "And it's all seen by no-one"

Chief Inspector Ramon Stompedo and his officer, Juan Abee, entered the restaurant, accompanied by Quantomundi, who had agreed to meet them at the retreat center.

Stompedo strode to the group's table and came right to the point. "Found a message on the answering machine this morning. Seems there was an unfortunate occurrence on the grounds here last night," he said, adding menacingly, "and possibly some foul play."

Quantomundi stepped forward, "I thought I made it clear in my message—it was an accident. Maya Llusion, a visiting workshop teacher, tripped and fell over the cliff's edge. We all witnessed it." He spread his arms to include the group at the table.

Stompedo, of course, knew of the respected shaman and was aware it would be folly to accuse him of lying. However, he plunged ahead. "Eduardo, the desk clerk, reports observing a wild scene on the cliff last night—high spirits, wild dancing. Smacks of drugs to me." He threw a challenging look at the shaman.

Quantomundi replied, "Only if you believe that a celebration of life is a crime. Everyone here can verify the account I have given you. There were no illegal drugs involved. And the unfortunate woman who disappeared was not part of this group last night."

Stompedo fumed, "Where is Neti Neti? He should be here!"

Bossy stood up. "Both Inspector Neti Neti and Sergeant Shadow saw it all and helped search for the body. We were some distance from the edge of the cliff. We saw her fall and ran to the cliff's edge to help, but it was too late. If you doubt us, ask your Inspector Neti Neti."

A frustrated Stompedo surveyed the serene group. Their calm detachment was unnerving, and he knew that without evidence or a body he was defeated. He turned and strode out of the building, hastily followed by Juan Abee.

The friends settled back and smiled at each other, beckoning Quantomundi to join them at the table. Beams of sunlight glinted off the crystal water glasses, mirroring the joyful twinkle in their eyes. The aroma of fresh coffee infused the air. The sound of the sea's endless motion...

And the play goes on.

Acknowledgements

We wish to express our heartfelt gratitude to Tony Parsons, of the United Kingdom, author of *As It Is*, for sharing the "open secret" with such clarity and refreshing humor.

We also wish to acknowledge our appreciation to Nancy Parker of Ashland Hills Press, our editor and publisher. Her dedication to our vision and her professional skill helped bring this book to fruition.

We are deeply grateful to our wonderful families and all our dear friends, who consistently held the field of potentiality open so that we could realize our dream.

About the Authors

Long-time friends, Diana Cooper and Judith Whitman-Small, gratefully acknowledge and celebrate the extraordinary journey they have shared in writing this book They have both studied the Enneagram for years and have been involved in the spiritual search for many more. In their travels throughout the world, they have enjoyed many colorful adventures, which have added flavor to their collaborative efforts.

A native Coloradoan, Diana received her B.A. degree in English from the University of Colorado. She has lived on Lookout Mountain west of Denver for a number of years.

Judith makes her home in Ashland, Oregon. She has a Masters degree in Psychology from The Institute of Transpersonal Psychology in Menlo Park, California.